Donovan was alive.

Raven had always believed she'd know if he wasn't, but recently she'd started to think her belief was simply misplaced hope. But he was alive and back living next door to her.

She gritted her teeth, holding back the angry scream that was fighting to get out. She'd held on to her love for all those years—worrying about him—and he'd been fine. Happy and healthy. She couldn't believe the man she'd loved had done that to her. But he had.

She'd waited for an explanation, hoping he'd give her a reason for vanishing from her life, but he hadn't even tried to explain. Maybe he thought he didn't owe her an explanation. Maybe she'd made more of their relationship than had actually been there. Perhaps she'd been the only one in love.

And now he was back. She couldn't allow him to consume her life again. It was clear now that she'd loved him more than he'd loved her. Apparently he'd said goodbye to her years ago. Well, now she'd said goodbye. She was engaged to another man and getting married in four weeks.

Even though she'd had Donovan's son.

* * *

SWEET BRIAR SWEETHEARTS:
There's something about Sweet Briar

Dear Reader,

Once again, I'm recommending a Harlequin Special Edition book to encourage readers to discover these compelling contemporary romances. The Special Edition line has always been full of great stories. The heroes and heroines are dynamic and relatable, trying their best to resist their attraction to each other while resolving the conflict that keeps them apart. But the undeniable chemistry that simmers between them cannot be denied. These books will pull you in and take you on an emotional and satisfying journey. Each story ends with a marriage proposal or wedding—delivering the happily-ever-after, because the love and security of family is the ultimate promise of Special Edition.

Kathy Douglass is one of Special Edition's newest voices. Her heartwarming stories portray a small town where everyone gets a warm welcome and a second chance. Sweet Briar, North Carolina, is a place where people come to heal and find community, friendship and even love. She pulls you right in from page one, and you won't want to leave.

This month's book is called *The Rancher's Return* and the story couldn't be juicier. After his life is no longer in danger, Donovan Cordero returns to his family ranch just outside Sweet Briar and finds out he has a son! Raven Reynolds is rightfully furious that Donovan has waltzed back into her life after ten years of silence, and the two of them have to figure out how they'll parent their child. Watching them come to terms with the past and build a life together in the present makes for a delightfully charming read.

All the best,

Paula Eykelhof Miller

The Rancher's
Return

—

Kathy Douglass

HARLEQUIN® SPECIAL EDITION

Recycling programs
for this product may
not exist in your area.

ISBN-13: 978-1-335-57374-2

The Rancher's Return

Copyright © 2019 by Kathleen Gregory

Printed in U.S.A.

Kathy Douglass came by her love of reading naturally—both of her parents were readers. She would finish one book and pick up another. Then she attended law school and traded romances for legal opinions.

After the birth of her two children, her love of reading turned into a love of writing. Kathy now spends her days writing the small-town contemporary novels she enjoys reading.

Books by Kathy Douglass

Harlequin Special Edition

Sweet Briar Sweethearts

How to Steal the Lawman's Heart
The Waitress's Secret
The Rancher and the City Girl
Winning Charlotte Back

To my husband and sons.
Thanks for your love and support. I love you all.

Chapter One

Everything looked the same. After ten years away, ten years when he'd wondered if he would ever see the ranch where he'd been born and raised again, Donovan Cordero was home.

He was surprised that not one thing had changed. The large house was still painted the white color his mother loved. The shutters were still black. The simple backdrop was perfect for showcasing the flower gardens on either side of the stairs where his mother had spent hours each day. His earliest memories were of pulling weeds beside her, learning how to care for a variety of plants and flowers.

When he'd gotten older he'd begun to trail his father around their one hundred seventy-five acre ranch. He'd felt guilty for turning his back on his mother, but when he'd apologize for leaving her behind and offer to stay with her, she'd only laugh and shoo him away. After spending the day learning how to care for horses and cows, he'd race into the house and to his mother, who would always give him a big hug and kiss. Later he'd begun hanging out with his three best friends, Tony Wilson, Billy Campbell and Jericho Jones on the Double J Ranch. No matter how late he returned, his mother was always waiting with open arms to welcome him home.

Would she be as welcoming now? She'd spent the past ten years believing he was dead.

Fearing for her life and those of others he'd loved, he'd let her go right on believing that. He'd been young and frightened back then, too afraid to think of any option other than running. After seeing Karl Rivers kill a man in cold blood, where could he turn? The sheriff? Not likely since the sheriff had been beside Rivers, watching the entire thing. No doubt he'd helped with the cover-up.

To this day he still remembered the fear that had filled him when they'd spotted him. He'd pleaded for his life, promising never to tell a soul what he'd seen. He'd thought for sure they were going to kill him. Then Rivers had lowered his gun. Rivers had told Donovan that since he had always protected his son Carson from bullies, he was going to let him live. But there was a condition: Donovan had to leave town immediately and never come back. If Donovan stayed in town or breathed a word of what he'd seen, Rivers would kill not only him and his parents, but his girlfriend, Raven Reynolds, too. The dead body on the ground in a pool of blood left no doubt that Rivers was serious. He'd kill them all.

Karl Rivers was a powerful man in the state of North

Carolina. A big political donor to Democrats and Republicans alike and cousin to the governor and a US senator, he had reach that Donovan could only imagine. As a teenage son of a simple rancher, Donovan had been no match for him. So he'd run. He'd left his parents and Raven behind for their good as well as his own.

Three days ago the major networks had carried the story of Rivers's death from a heart attack. Donovan had watched in anger as politicians from one end of the country to the other gave tribute to Rivers, speaking of him in glowing terms. No one would ever know what a monster he'd been. But then a sense of relief replaced the anger. Donovan could go home without risking the lives of those he loved.

So he'd quit his job on the ranch where he'd worked under a fake name for the past seven years. Though he liked Della and Gabe Turner, he didn't give them the notice he would have if he were leaving for any other reason. He'd wanted to get home as soon as possible. He'd said goodbye to the men and women on the cattle ranch who had become his friends, loaded up his truck and driven east.

He checked his watch. Five fifty-eight. He'd been sitting in his truck for the past three minutes. Now that he was home, his knees felt weak and his heart thudded in his chest. He'd been in the area for almost ten minutes but he'd driven around trying to get rid of his sudden anxiety. He'd been fine as he'd driven Interstate 20 across several states. But as he'd crossed into North Carolina, he'd gotten anxious. The closer he got to home, the more jittery he'd become.

Dinner had always been at six o'clock in the Cordero home. Donovan's mother had designated that hour as family time and it was sacred; Donovan's father had never once been late, no matter how much work remained. So Donovan knew he was about to see both of his parents within a matter of minutes.

Breathing hard, Donovan got out of the car and sprinted across the driveway and up the stairs. Never in the nineteen years that he'd lived in this house had he rung the doorbell and it felt strange to do it now. But after being gone all these years, he didn't feel right strolling into the house and asking what was for dinner. As the doorbell pealed, his heart sped up. He heard footsteps. As they got closer, his anticipation grew.

"Yes?"

At the sound of his mother's beloved voice his eyes filled with tears. He looked through the screen door. "Ma?"

His mother gasped. Visibly shaken, she staggered back. For a second he thought she might pass out, but with a strength he remembered, she grasped the door and stared. Tears filled her eyes and ran down her smooth, brown cheeks. "Donovan. Oh, my sweet baby boy. You're home. My baby boy is home."

He yanked open the door and pulled his sobbing mother into his arms. "I'm home, Ma. I'm home."

"Lena, who is that showing up at dinnertime?" Donovan's dad asked, coming into the entryway.

Donovan looked up, not releasing his mother from their embrace. "It's me, Dad."

Donovan's father stared at him for a moment. The look on his face was that of a man whose every dream had just come true. He gave a shout of joy then crossed the room in long strides, taking Donovan and his mother into his arms. "Son. You're home. I've waited ten long years for this day to come."

As the family hugged, a sense of relief and joy that had been a decade in the making filled Donovan. They held on to each other for long minutes before separating. They didn't fully break contact but rather leaned on each other as they walked into the living room and sat on the familiar striped sofa his mother had fallen in love with on sight at the store.

Donovan took a quick look around the room. Everything was blessedly familiar. The furniture was in the exact same arrangement as it had been when he'd last seen it if a bit more worn. The same family photographs hung over the fireplace, freezing them in time.

"I knew you would come home," his mother said, dabbing at the corner of her eyes with the hem of her white blouse. "Everyone told us that you were dead and that we needed to move on, but I knew better. I knew you were alive. A mother's heart knows."

"As does a father's."

Watery laughter burst from Donovan's mouth. Mario Cordero had always insisted that a father could love just as strongly as a mother and that a dad possessed the same intuition when it came to his children.

"And you're just in time for dinner." Donovan's mother rose and, grabbing his hand, led him to the kitchen.

After washing his hands, Donovan sat at the familiar table in his usual seat. There was something comforting about having everything the same as he remembered. His mother had made a roast with vegetables, one of his favorite meals. He had to admit that no matter what she'd made, he would have been ecstatic. Over the years he'd eaten at many tables, but nothing compared to sitting down at this scarred oak table again.

As they ate, they talked about everything and nothing. They were too emotional to have deep conversations and frequently wiped happy tears from their faces. When the meal had been eaten, they lingered into the night, sipping sweet coffee. Until finally they could no longer avoid the burning question that had so far gone unasked.

"Why did you leave, son?" Lena asked quietly, heartbreak and confusion in her voice.

Donovan had known this time would come. He'd prepared many answers that he hoped would satisfy them without bringing up the terrible past. Now that he was face-to-face with his parents, seeing the love in their eyes, he couldn't lie to them. He respected them too much. Besides, after years of worry, they deserved the truth. "I saw something I shouldn't have. A murder. The man who committed the crime threatened us and Raven if I didn't leave town immediately. So I left."

"Oh my God," Lena whispered.

"Are you safe now?" Mario asked, rising. No doubt he was going for one of the guns he kept locked in a gun safe in his study.

"I believe so. The murderer is dead now."

"I never heard anything about a murder back then." Mario sank back into his seat. "Why didn't you come to me? We could have gone to the sheriff."

Donovan shook his head then stared at his father. "No, we couldn't have."

It only took a second for that to sink in.

"I always knew that man was a snake," Mario said, anger filling his voice. "No wonder he died under suspicious circumstances three years ago. There's no telling how many crimes he covered up."

"It doesn't matter now," Lena said, patting Donovan's cheek like she'd done when he was a kid. "You're home and that's all I care about."

Donovan knew that once the euphoria and shock of his return wore off, his parents would ask more questions. Even now Donovan sensed there was more his father wanted to ask but mercifully he held back. Emotionally drained, Donovan was grateful for the reprieve.

A somber feeling settled in the room, taking some of the glow from the earlier joy and excitement of Donovan's return. A few minutes passed before Lena jumped up. "You must be tired. Your room is all set."

Donovan was tired but he was much too keyed up to sleep. Nevertheless he followed his parents to his room. The door was closed but when he opened it, it was like stepping into the past. His room was exactly the way he'd left it. If not for the fact that he'd lived every single day, Donovan might have believed the past ten years had been a mirage. The only thing different was the bare mattress. His mother grabbed some sheets from the linen closet and headed for the bed.

"I can do that, Ma," Donovan said, reaching for the sheets.

"I know you can. But I've come into this room for years, longing for the day you would return and sleep in this bed again. Let me make it for you."

When she put it like that, there was no way Donovan could say no, so he stepped aside and let his mother put sheets on his bed. While she worked, he moved around his room, touching mementos from his youth. He'd never been especially neat, and everything remained as he'd left it. His computer was still centered on his desk, along with a comic book, open to the exact page where he'd stopped reading.

"Done," his mother said, beaming at him.

"Thanks, Ma." He pulled his mother into a tight hug then walked with her to the door. She hadn't tucked him in since he was about seven or eight, but he could tell she would be happy to do so tonight if he'd let her. Instead he kissed her on her forehead and told her how glad he was to be home again. "See you guys in the morning."

After they hugged him one more time, Donovan's parents said good-night and he closed the door behind them. Once he was alone in his room, Donovan picked up a picture from his bookcase. Raven. His heart skipped a beat as he looked at the girl he'd loved from the time he was sixteen. With clear brown skin and large, dark eyes, she'd been a beauty. Her long, thick hair was a rich black, befitting her name.

Her parents owned the neighboring ranch, so they'd grown up together. For the first years of his life, he'd thought of Raven as one of the guys. Their mothers had been close friends so he and Raven had played together from the time they could walk. When he'd been about nine or ten, he and his three best friends had formed a boys only club and Raven had been excluded. He could still remember the tears in her eyes when he'd told her that boys and girls didn't play together so they couldn't be friends anymore.

When he turned sixteen, he'd seen Raven riding her horse along the fence that separated their property. He'd called out to her but she'd ridden away. He'd tried to catch up with her but she'd been a magnificent rider and left him in the dust. Captivated by her beauty, he'd been determined to re-establish their friendship. Two days later he'd gotten up the nerve to show up at her home unannounced. She hadn't been impressed. In fact, she hadn't even acknowledged his presence until he'd given her a bouquet of pink roses. Then she'd smiled and his heart had leaped.

They'd sat on her front porch for hours that day. He'd accepted her mother's invitation to dinner. When he'd gone home that evening, he'd been totally in love and known that she was the girl he'd marry. Raven hadn't been convinced of his sincerity and he'd had to work hard to win her heart. By the time summer ended, he'd succeeded. They'd been inseparable until the day he'd been forced to leave her behind.

Was she married now? The youngest of five children, she'd wanted a bunch of kids of her own. No doubt she had a family by now. Just because his parents appeared to have remained frozen in time waiting for him to return didn't mean that Raven had.

Donovan pulled back the curtains and stared out the window. The full moon and bright stars illuminated the night. Suddenly he yearned to see more of the ranch. Tiptoeing down the stairs so as not to disturb his parents, he grabbed his boots from the front hall and carried them until he was standing on the back porch. He quickly put them on and headed for the stables.

He pulled the doors open and looked around then walked slowly down the center aisle. When he reached the third stall he stopped. Zeus. His horse. He'd gotten Zeus for his fifteenth birthday. Some kids liked dogs and treated them like family, but Zeus had been all he'd wanted.

He reached out and rubbed his horse's nose. Zeus snorted and then began stomping his feet, pawing at the floor in his excitement. Once the horse calmed down, Donovan led him out of the stall and quickly saddled him. Donovan put his foot into the stirrup and swung into the saddle.

The night was quiet and Donovan relaxed as he started across the moonlit grass toward the open fields. He and Zeus had traveled this way many nights. When he and Raven had been dating, they'd had a special place where they'd meet at night. It was on Cordero land but close enough to the Reynolds' ranch that Raven could ride there easily. They'd rendezvous beside a babbling brook then wander hand-in-hand through the meadow. Donovan had carved their initials on the trunk of one of the many large trees. He'd told her it was a sign that he'd regretted all the ways that he'd hurt her in the past and a vow that he'd love her forever. It hadn't been an original idea, but Raven had been so moved that she'd actually cried.

But then Raven had always worn her heart on her sleeve. There had never been any mystery to her heart or how she'd felt. She'd never played games so he had never felt the need to do so, either.

As he neared the meadow, he heard the sound of hooves. The sound was faint, but he caught a glimpse of someone riding away. The rider was too far off for Donovan to tell if the person was a man or woman. When he reached his destination, he put it out of his mind. He was there to reconnect with a special piece of land and to see if he could recapture some of the joy he'd felt back then.

Dismounting, Donovan walked to the tree. Though it had been a decade since he'd been here last, he could have found the spot where he'd carved a heart with their initials while blindfolded. He rubbed his hand over the letters and then sat. He'd visit Raven's family ranch tomorrow and find out how she was doing. He didn't expect to rekindle their relationship after all this time, but it would be good to catch up with her.

The horse neighed and Donovan rose. He needed to get back to the house. Ranch work started early and Donovan wanted to help out his dad the way he always had, so he mounted the horse and headed for home.

Raven Reynolds crept into the kitchen, hoping to get to her room without running into anyone. Not that she'd done anything wrong. She just didn't feel like having a discussion with her mother about where she'd been. Marilyn Reynolds was nobody's fool and she could put two and two together faster than anyone. And really, there was no mystery about where Raven had been. She'd been caught coming in from meeting Donovan many times when she'd been a teenager. They'd loved each other so deeply they couldn't bear to be apart for an entire night.

But then he'd vanished without a trace ten years ago. Every rancher in the area and citizen of Sweet Briar, the nearest town, had looked for him, but they'd never turned up a clue. It was as if Donovan had existed one day then ceased existing the next. Despite evidence to the contrary, she'd believed in her heart he was alive and would return to her. Even now she refused to believe he was dead.

But even so, it was time to move on. She'd finally accepted that even if he was still alive somewhere, he was not returning home. As much as she loved him, it was time to say goodbye to him. She thought she'd done that when she'd accepted Carson Rivers's marriage proposal five months ago. She'd been wrong. A part of her had still been holding on to Donovan and the future they'd dreamed of sharing. That future wasn't going to happen. If she was going to be true to Carson and give their marriage a chance, she needed to actually say goodbye to Donovan for good.

So tonight she'd ridden out to their special place on his family ranch and watched as the sun set and the moon rose. Memory after memory flashed through her mind and she'd shed more than a few tears. She'd ranted and raved at the injustice of it all, releasing the pain she hadn't been able to get rid of in all these years. When she'd been worn out emotionally, she'd gotten on her horse and ridden home.

Thankfully no one was in the kitchen and she was able to make it upstairs without discovery. She looked in at Elias and found that he'd fallen asleep while reading again. She turned off the flashlight and put a bookmark on the page before putting the book on his nightstand. It was a hassle to get him to do his math homework, but he willingly read at least two books a week, not including comic books that he read by the half dozen. She kissed her son on the forehead then crossed his room, closing the door behind her.

When Raven reached her room, she flung herself across her bed and began to sob. She thought she'd cried her last tears when she'd run her hand across the carved letters on their tree, but she'd been wrong. There were still tears left. But as she let them come, she vowed that this would be the last time. She needed to commit one hundred percent to her fiancé and to put Donovan Cordero in the past.

Chapter Two

"I want to have a party," Lena said, putting three slices of bacon on Donovan's already overflowing plate. He'd awakened at the crack of dawn and gotten dressed to help his father with morning chores. His mother had been awake, as well, humming as she bustled around the kitchen. She'd always made a hearty breakfast for them, but this was above and beyond anything she'd prepared in the past.

"What kind of party?" Donovan asked then held up a hand preventing his mother from adding fried ham to his plate.

"For the neighbors and the people of Sweet Briar. I want to let everyone know that you're back home." Lena sat and began eating her own food. "Maybe we can have a cookout this weekend."

Donovan chewed for a while, pondering how best

to turn down his mother. He understood her enthusi-
asm, but he wasn't ready for that kind of interaction
with the community just yet. Actually he would prefer
not to make a big deal of his return. He'd rather handle
people one-on-one as he encountered them. "Maybe
later. I'm not really up to seeing the whole town right
now. I'd like to settle down a bit and spend time with
my family and closest friends for a while."

"I'm just so happy you're home. I want to tell the
whole world."

"I'm not saying keep it a secret. You can tell anyone
you want. I just don't want to be around a whole lot of
people right now."

His mother sighed, disappointed.

"Lena, let the boy settle in first," Mario said, patting Donovan's mother on the hand. "Think of this time
as ours alone. And in the meantime you can plan the
biggest party this county has ever seen for when he is
ready."

"All right," Lena conceded, to Donovan's great relief. "A good party will require planning."

They talked more as they ate. When Mario finished eating, he stood and Donovan did, as well. He'd
spent the past ten years as a paid hand on other people's ranches. He'd worked hard, earning every cent he'd
been paid. It felt good to work just as hard on land that
belonged to his family. "See you at lunch."

Donovan worked beside his father and the ranch
hands. He only recognized one or two of them from
before he'd left. The rest his father had hired over the
years. Mario paid a fair wage and expected his men
to earn it. It was only after he'd been on his own and

working for others that Donovan appreciated the way his father managed his employees.

After dinner Donovan felt restless. He tried to fight it, but after a few minutes of an intense internal battle gave up. He needed to see Raven. Grabbing his keys and hat, he told his parents he'd be back later and drove up the road to the Reynolds' property. For all he knew, she could have moved away as her older brothers had. Or as much as he hated the thought, she could be married with kids. He should have asked his parents. Well, it was too late now. If she no longer lived there, her parents could tell him how to get in touch with her.

Though each of the ranches was a decent size, the ride by truck only took ten minutes. During that short drive, Donovan recalled the last time he'd seen Raven. They'd met at their special spot. She'd been anxious to tell him something and he hadn't been able to determine whether she'd been excited or scared. His friend Billy had been home on leave from the army and he'd phoned Donovan before Raven could share her secret. He'd been willing to stay with her, but she'd encouraged him to hang out with his friend. He'd promised to come to her house later so they could talk. Then he'd witnessed the murder and his life had been irrevocably changed. If he could turn back time, he would have stayed with Raven.

Over the years, when he'd been especially lonely for home, he'd wondered what Raven had wanted to tell him. He'd imagined all sorts of things but doubted he'd ever come close to the truth. He supposed he could ask her now but he wouldn't. Ten years had passed. Though the moment had been indelibly marked in his mind, he doubted it was the same for her. For all intents and purposes, his life had ended when he'd left town. Hers had not.

He pulled into the circle drive in front of the large ranch house where Raven had grown up. Unlike his parents, the Reynolds had made changes to their home. The porch swing where he and Raven had spent many pleasant evenings had been replaced by dark brown wicker furniture with floral pillows. A wooden chest with a padded top was centered in front of the love seat.

As he waited for someone to answer the door, it occurred to him that this was the second time in as many days that he was standing on someone's porch waiting to tell them he was alive. For a moment he thought about leaving, but decided that ten years was long enough to go without seeing Raven. Besides, no matter how she found out, she was going to be shocked. And he'd missed her too much to wait. Over the years he'd dated other women, but he'd never given his heart to any of them. He'd been living a lie and hadn't been in a position to be honest with anyone without risking their lives, too. If he'd had to leave town suddenly, he couldn't have taken anyone with him. He hadn't wanted to risk the pain of separation again. Though time had passed and his feelings had faded, Raven was the only girl he'd ever loved.

The door swung open and there she was. *Raven.* His heart stuttered and all he could do was stare.

She was even more beautiful than he remembered. More beautiful than in his dreams. Tall and skinny when they'd been teenagers, she'd filled out and now had slim curves. Her straight black hair hung over her shoulders, gently caressing her breasts. But it was her face with her big brown eyes, high cheekbones and full lips that captivated him.

"Hi. Can I help you?" Though she looked at him quizzically, she smiled.

His breath caught in his throat and he lost the power to speak. Over the years he'd imagined seeing her again and thought of what he'd say. How he'd feel. But he'd underestimated the emotion that would consume him as he finally came face-to-face with the girl he'd loved. His vision blurred and he blinked away the moisture in his eyes. Time had intervened and he no longer loved her the way he had at nineteen, but there was still an unnamable *something* there. A connection that had compelled him to see her even though she'd surely moved on with her life.

"Sir? Are you okay?"

Donovan had no idea how much time had passed but it had been enough to arouse her concern. "Raven."

She gasped and looked at him. *Really* looked. "Don—Donovan?"

"Yes."

The color drained from her face and she froze. Then her entire body began to shake. She reached out her arms and slowly began to sag to the floor. Donovan stepped inside and managed to catch her before she hit the floor. He scooped her into his arms and carried her into the front room and lay her on her sofa.

How could he be so stupid? Showing up out of the blue was boneheaded and inconsiderate. After ten years without hearing from him, she had to believe he was dead. He should have anticipated this kind of reaction. Even his mother, who'd never given up hope that he'd return, had nearly fainted with shock at the sight of him.

He should have let his mother throw the party like she'd wanted. That way nobody would react as if they'd seen a ghost when they saw him. He'd told his mother she could tell whomever she wanted that he was back, but he didn't know who she'd told so far. Not that it mattered now. Clearly the word hadn't reached Raven.

Her hair had fallen over her face and he brushed it aside then watched, waiting for her to come around. After a minute her eyelashes fluttered and she began to stir. She opened her eyes and stared right at him then lifted her hand and touched his face. "It's really you."

"It's really me."

She pushed herself into a sitting position then scooted around and put her feet on the floor. She was still wobbly although her color was returning.

"Easy."

Raven reached out and wrapped her arms around him. He inhaled her familiar scent. She smelled of outdoors and sunshine with a slight hint of lavender soap. He closed his eyes and simply enjoyed the feel of her. Although their bodies had changed and matured over the past decade, she still fit perfectly in his arms.

After a moment she pulled back slightly and looked into his eyes. The joy he saw in her gaze was unmistakable. "When did you get back?"

"Yesterday. Dinnertime."

She touched his face again as if trying to convince herself that he was real. "You came back yesterday?"

He nodded.

"Where have you been all this time?"

"Working on ranches in Texas."

"But you never called. You never came back." She sounded confused. Hurt.

He could imagine that she felt angry and betrayed, among other things. At least that's what he would feel in her position. He'd known this wasn't going to be an easy conversation, but it was more difficult than he'd expected. The heartbroken expression on her face seared his soul.

"I'm back now." He wished he had the words to take away her pain but he didn't think they existed. He wanted to tell her the truth, but she was so shaky he didn't think she could handle the shock of discovering her life had been threatened. He would tell her the truth when she was stronger.

She snorted. "That's all you have to say? You're back now?"

She pushed to her feet then stumbled. He immediately grabbed her elbow to steady her. Her weakness only steeled his resolve to protect her. A body could only take so much and obviously she couldn't handle another emotional blow now.

"I guess. It's good to see you."

She jerked away. "You need to leave. Now."

"Raven."

"Do you have any idea how worried I was? How scared? The entire town searched for you day and night. Jericho, Tony and Billy drove back and forth to town for weeks looking for clues that would help us find you. Your parents put up fliers. The church held fund-raisers to raise money for a reward. They raised twenty-five-thousand dollars for information. Mr. Rivers contributed twenty-five-thousand dollars so we would have a fifty-thousand-dollar reward."

Donovan stiffened at Karl Rivers's name. That old hypocrite, pretending to care about Donovan. No doubt he thought it was best to keep track of what was being done to find him. Not to mention it made him look good. Having a good public image made it that much easier to do his dirt in the dark. That and owning politicians and controlling law enforcement.

"Do you know how many nights I couldn't sleep because I was worrying about you? Praying for you? I cried for months. I had to force myself to eat because of... I was devastated. Everyone kept telling me that you were dead, but I didn't believe it. I kept hoping you would come back to me. As time passed without a word, I figured you must have been hurt. That was the only reason I could think of that you wouldn't return to me. I promised God that I would take care of you if he'd only bring you back. And all the time you've been fine. You could have come home if you'd wanted. You just didn't want to."

"That's not true." He hadn't meant to justify his actions, but hearing her speak as if she hadn't been his entire world was unbearable. He would have sacrificed his life to come back. He just hadn't been willing to sacrifice hers.

"Were you in prison? In a coma? Held hostage?"

He'd been held hostage but not in the way Raven meant. His love for her and his family had made it impossible to return as long as Karl Rivers lived. But as soon as the news of the man's death reached him, Donovan had been freed from his captivity. He'd barely stopped to sleep or eat on his race to get home.

"Well?" Raven pressed.

There would be no reasoning with her tonight. Not unless he was willing to shock her further by telling her about the threat to her life. He didn't want to win the argument that badly.

"No. I was none of those things."

Raven forced herself not to cry at Donovan's words. She thought of all the years she'd spent hoping he would come home. She'd never believed he would leave her without a good reason, so she'd figured something had to be wrong with him. There just had to be a reason he hadn't returned to her. She'd tried to put herself in his mind and come up with an explanation for his prolonged absence. As time went on, her reasons became more desperate.

Perhaps he'd been badly injured. Maybe he'd been disfigured or paralyzed and thought she wouldn't love him any longer. But she'd love Donovan no matter what. She'd prayed that God could reach him wherever he was and help him to know that.

Other times she'd imagine he had amnesia and had forgotten who he was and where he belonged. She'd searched online for stories about young men found without identification and police looking for help from the public. Over the years she'd read about three or four such cases, but none had been the man she'd loved with her whole heart and soul. She'd been dying inside, and he'd been fine and dandy, living his life in Texas.

How could he do that to her? And his parents? The Corderos had been destroyed. With the passage of time, they'd become more distraught, barely able to care for themselves. After a while other people moved on with their lives, putting Donovan's disappearance in the past as a mystery that might never be solved. Mr. and Mrs.

Cordero had been the only ones who'd shared Raven's belief that Donovan would one day return.

"Did your parents know where you were?" It would be awful to think that they'd betrayed her the way he had.

"No. No one knew where I was."

"Well, at least I know you were just as cruel to them as you were to me."

"Don't cry, Raven. I didn't come here to hurt you."

She angrily wiped at tears she hadn't realized were falling. "Then why did you come?"

He seemed to mull that over. That was different. The Donovan of her youth had been impulsive and fun. A daredevil, he'd act first and think later. He'd changed. And not just his personality.

He was physically different, too.

Ten years ago he'd been tall and lanky. Being a ranch kid, he'd been physically strong even if he hadn't had the muscles as evidence. He was still the same height, probably six feet two or three, but his shoulders were broader and his chest was fuller, yet his stomach was just as flat, his waist as trim. If his muscular body was anything to go by, whatever he'd been doing had been physical. His brown skin glowed with good health and his eyes were clear and sharp as ever. From all appearances, he'd lived well this past decade.

That thought pierced her soul. He could have returned to her and had chosen not to. Instead he'd been living the good life in Texas. Not that she'd wanted him to have suffered. The thought of him in agony somewhere was more than her heart could take. But knowing that he'd left her in misery for ten long years when he hadn't had to shred her heart. She would never forgive him.

And to think she'd dreamed of this moment for years. None of her imaginings had looked like this. And they certainly hadn't hurt like this. Nothing could ever hurt this badly. "You need to leave. Now."

"I'm sorry for hurting you. I hope we can become friends again."

Friends? Not likely. She hated him. If she never saw him again, it would be too soon. As far as she was concerned he could disappear forever. He'd kept his existence a secret for years. If he wanted to keep secrets... well she could do the same. "No. We're done."

She heard the pounding of feet a second before she heard the voice. And then she knew she wouldn't be able to keep her secret after all.

"Mom?"

Chapter Three

Mom? Donovan reeled at the word. Did Raven have a child? A husband? Although he'd told himself he wanted her to have moved on and made a happy life without him, the thought that she'd fallen in love with another man sucked the air from his lungs. He didn't even try to reconcile the two opposing feelings. Emotions weren't logical and it would be foolish to try to make sense of them.

He turned to see a boy of about eight or nine standing there looking straight at Raven. When she didn't answer him, he directed his attention to Donovan. "Who are you?"

Donovan opened his mouth to answer but when he met the kid's eyes he couldn't speak. His stomach seized as if he'd been punched in the gut. The kid's eyes were the exact shade of gray as the ones that stared at Donovan from the mirror each morning as he shaved. The same gray eyes Donovan had inherited from his father. Realization dawned fast and Donovan's knees buckled. *This boy was his son.* Raven had been pregnant and he hadn't known it. Was that what she'd planned to tell him that last day?

"Who is he, Mom?"

Donovan wanted to blurt out that he was his father but he didn't. That would be selfish. For all Donovan knew, Raven was married and the kid might believe his stepfather was his dad. Was Raven married? Donovan looked at her left hand. No ring. Not that the absence of a wedding band meant anything. She could have taken it off to do work around the ranch. Or maybe she'd simply forgotten to put it on this morning. There were any number of reasons to explain why Raven wasn't wearing a ring.

Raven glanced at Donovan before smiling at the boy. "This is Donovan Cordero. He's Mr. and Mrs. Cordero's son and a friend of mine."

"Mr. and Mrs. Cordero are nice." His eyes lit up and he took a step closer to Donovan. "Are you the guy who disappeared?"

Donovan managed a nod.

"Wow. Where were you? Why didn't you come home?"

"Elias. Enough with the questions. What did you want with me?"

Elias grinned and a dimple flashed in his left cheek. Donovan also had a dimple in his left cheek. It was like seeing himself at nine years old. "I wanted to tell you there's going to be a carnival in Sweet Briar this weekend and ask if you want to go with me."

Raven smiled. "If I want to go with you? That's a pretty sneaky question since I don't remember saying you could go."

"Oh, Mom. All the kids are going. Please."

"I'll decide after I see the grade on your math test."

"Mom."

Raven cut off Elias mid-grumble. "I need to talk to Donovan. Go start your homework."

"Okay." The boy took two steps then turned back around and grinned at Donovan. "Welcome home."

"Thanks," Donovan said but the kid had already sprinted from the room.

Neither Raven nor Donovan spoke for a minute. Donovan was in a state of shock and incapable of forming a coherent sentence. The world had completely tilted and he was struggling to get it back on its axis. Adding the new revelation to the emotional upheaval of the past five days had left him emotionally wrung out. He tried to grab hold of his rapidly shifting emotions but couldn't get a handle on even one of them. Two thoughts kept circling his mind. *I have a son. And he doesn't know who I am.*

He blew out a breath and then looked at Raven. Though she'd managed to hold it together while Elias was in the room, she was trembling again. She looked as weak as he felt.

He reached out a hand to her. "Raven."

Her eyes filled with tears as she met his gaze. "What?"

"He's mine, isn't he? Elias is my son." Although he'd known the second he'd seen the child, he needed to hear her say it.

"Yes." That softly spoken word changed his entire life. He was a father.

He smiled. "Thank you."

"For what?"

"For having my son. You didn't have to. I know it couldn't have been easy for you."

Surprise had her deep brown eyes widening. "You're not upset?"

"Upset? No. Why would I be?"

"Because." She gave a nervous laugh. "I don't know. Back then I was so afraid you'd be angry at me for getting pregnant. I worried you might think I was trying to trap you. I guess that feeling popped up now because... I don't know."

Donovan *was* angry. But not at Raven. She'd given him a son. He was angry at Karl Rivers. Because of him Donovan had been a father for nine years and not known it. He'd missed watching Raven grow bigger as their child grew within her and then holding her hand as she'd given birth to their son. He'd missed every day of his son's life. All because of Karl Rivers.

Anger at the man consumed Donovan and nearly bubbled over. He suppressed it. He couldn't let his fury show. If he did, Raven would believe he was angry at her.

"Are you married?"

"What?"

"Are you married? Do you have a husband? Other kids?"

Raven took two steps and got in his face. Her eyes flashed with fury although he couldn't imagine why she was angry. It was a logical question. "You have your nerve. You vanish, leaving me pregnant and alone and out of my mind worrying about what could be happening to you. And you were fine. You could have come home anytime. You could have called to let me know you were alive and well. But you didn't care enough about what I was going through to do that. So you don't get to know about my life. It's none of your business."

"It is, too, my business. Elias is my son. If some other man is around him, I have a right to know."

"A right?" She sputtered and her hands fisted. He'd never known Raven to be violent but a lot could have changed in ten years. Even though he doubted her personality had changed that much, he didn't want to test that theory, so he took a step back.

"Yes. I'm Elias's father." Raven sucked in a breath and Donovan spoke quickly before she could get wound up again. "I'm not saying this the right way."

"No kidding."

"Let me try again. I'm still in a state of shock here, so if I'm fumbling for words, I apologize."

"You're not the only one. I'm reeling myself."

"I'm grateful to you for having my son. For raising him. I don't know enough words to tell you how much. But he's my son, too, and I want the opportunity to be a part of his life. I want to get to know him. Spend time with him."

She shook her head. "So you think you're just going to waltz back into town and into Elias's life and act as if you haven't been missing in action for the past decade? Is that what you're saying?"

"I know I haven't been a part of Elias's life, but I want to be. I'm back now."

"For how long?"

"I'm staying."

Raven put a hand on her forehead. He wished he could know what she was thinking but maybe it was best that he couldn't. His head was so full that he didn't think he could hold another thought. "I haven't seen or heard from you in ten years, Donovan. Ten years. Surely you don't expect me to just let you hang out with my son. I don't trust you that much. Or at all, really. For all I know, you could take my son and vanish for another ten years."

"Our son. And no. I don't expect you to let me take him places. At least not yet. But I do want to get to know him."

She paced the room for several stressful minutes. Finally she looked at him. Her expression was firm, her eyes steel. "I'm not going to tell him who you are right now. That's not debatable."

Donovan was disappointed at Raven's pronouncement but squashed the urge to fight with her. She already harbored animosity for what she believed was his callous disregard of her feelings. Arguing with her over this wouldn't help. So he'd allow her to make the rules for now. Besides, it might be easier to get to know Elias if he didn't know Donovan's true identity. He might resent Donovan for being absent all of his life. It might be better to build a relationship than to tell Elias the truth. That way, if Elias was upset, they would have established a bond, making it easier to deal with his feelings.

"Okay."

"And another thing. You aren't going to be alone with Elias. If you're with him, then so am I. Again, that's not negotiable."

Donovan nodded, keeping himself from smiling. He'd often thought of Raven over the years. On those endless, lonely nights when he'd longed to come home, memories of time they'd spent together kept him going. Though he'd never stopped hoping he'd be able to come home one day, he'd never let himself believe he and Raven would ever be together again. Now she was insisting on it. He knew she wasn't saying they spend time together because she missed him or wanted to take up where they left off. She didn't trust him. Still he was anticipating the next few days and weeks. "Okay. So when can I see him again?"

She breathed out a sigh. She looked drained. "I don't know, Donovan. You've shaken up my life. You're back from the dead and wanting to be a part of our son's life. I need a minute to think about things and get my bearings."

"That's fair." Truth be told, although he wanted to start spending time with his son and Raven immediately, he needed to get his bearings, too. He'd gone from trying to catch up with his first love to discovering he was a father in under an hour. Not to mention that he was home again, his exile over. Sure the changes in his life were all positive, but he still could use time to process everything.

"I'll call you in a couple of days and we can set up something."

"Okay." He gave her his cell phone number and had her call him so he'd have her number, too. Once they'd saved each other's info, she walked out of the room in a none-too-subtle hint that it was time for him to leave. When they reached the door, she held it open. Before he stepped through it he touched her hand. Their eyes met and held. "Thanks again for my son."

* * *

Raven watched from the window as Donovan walked to his truck. She needed to make sure he didn't turn around and come back. She had to make sure he was gone before she loosened the reins on her emotions. Only after he'd driven away did she allow herself to sag into a chair.

Donovan was alive. She'd always believed she'd know if he wasn't, but recently she'd started to think her belief was simply misplaced hope. But he was alive and living next door to her. Lucky for her next door in a ranching community didn't mean the same thing as it did in a town. He couldn't see her as she came and went about her day so she'd still have the privacy necessary to maintain some semblance of order in her life.

Order in her life. That was a joke. Her life had spun out of control the moment she'd opened the door and seen Donovan standing on the other side. It had been a dream come true until it wasn't.

She gritted her teeth, holding back the angry scream that was fighting to get out. She'd held on to her love for all those years—worrying about him—and he'd been fine. Happy and healthy. She couldn't believe the man she'd loved had done that to her. But he had.

She'd waited for an explanation, hoping he'd give her a reason for vanishing from her life, but he hadn't even tried to explain. Perhaps because there wasn't a reason for hurting her that way. Or maybe he thought he didn't owe her an explanation. Maybe she'd made more of their relationship than had actually been there. Perhaps she'd been the only one in love.

She needed to get out of there. The minute her parents got home from the grocery store, Raven asked her mother to keep an eye on Elias then she saddled Evening Dream, her favorite horse, and headed across the grass to a spot she knew she wouldn't be disturbed. When she and Donovan had been young and in love, they'd spent blissful hours in their special place. Once he'd disappeared, she couldn't go there without thinking of him and breaking down, so she'd found a new location where she could have a bit of peace. Somewhere she didn't associate with Donovan. She'd ridden her entire ranch until she'd found a field where her soul felt at rest. It was as far away from the Cordero ranch as she could get while staying on her property. That's where she headed now.

Evening Dream seemed to instinctively know where Raven wanted to go, so she let her mind wander as the horse crossed the ranch at a leisurely pace. When they reached the boulder where Raven frequently sat to think, she dismounted and let Evening Dream drink from a nearby spring. Rather than sit, Raven picked up long blades of grass and began to split them. When the silence became too much for her, she leaned back, lifted her head and let out a long scream, voicing all of the stress, confusion and pain churning inside her. Her yell startled several birds, sending them flying from their tree and across the cloudless sky. Evening Dream looked up and stamped her foot in disapproval before resuming her drink.

Raven brushed hair out of her face and was surprised to discover moisture on her cheeks. Sinking to the ground, she began to sob in earnest. She wasn't exactly sure why she was crying, but she knew part of her sorrow had to do with the time she'd lost. Ten long years had come and gone and she'd been so consumed with fear and worry and undying hope for Donovan's return that she'd barely experienced any of them. Life had passed her by.

She loved her son and did everything in her power to be a good mother to him. The first couple of years had been especially trying and she was honest enough to know she'd been a basket case and not the parent Elias had needed. Fortunately her mother and father had filled the gap, giving their grandson all the love and attention he'd needed. Her parents had constantly urged her to stop wandering around like a ghost and give Elias her full attention. She hadn't had the strength. It wasn't until she'd heard Elias call her mother "Mommy" that Raven had begun to focus on her son.

But when the night came and Elias was safely asleep, she'd let her mind wander down the road to the secret place in her heart where Donovan lived. In the quiet midnight hour, she'd write letters to him that she knew he would never get. She'd done that every night until two days ago when she'd realized that to go forward she needed to put the past behind her. She was engaged to a good man who deserved all of her heart.

And now Donovan was back. She couldn't allow him to consume her life again. It was clear now that she'd loved him more than he'd loved her. Apparently he'd said goodbye to her years ago. Well now she'd said goodbye. She was engaged to another man and getting married in four weeks. Donovan might be back in town but he was out of her life. He was part of her past and that was where she intended for him to stay.

Chapter Four

"I think I'll sit outside for a while," Raven said to her parents, who were sitting in the living room. Following her breakdown in the meadow, Raven had ridden back to the ranch and helped her mother clean up the dinner dishes. She'd expected her mother to ask her about Donovan's visit, but she hadn't said a blessed word. Marilyn must have known Raven wasn't up to talking about it because she'd kept the conversation light.

That extended to the hour before Elias's bath time, when he'd dominated the conversation, talking about his plans for summer vacation. What he'd conveniently overlooked was that there were two more weeks of school, including final exams. She'd checked his homework and was pleased that he'd gotten all of his math problems correct. She let him read for half an hour before going to sleep each night, so after he selected one of the three books he was reading simultaneously, she'd set the timer for thirty minutes and reminded him to go to sleep when it went off. She'd picked up a stray sock and tossed it into his hamper then joined her parents in the living room.

"Carson not coming over tonight?" her father asked her as she headed outside.

"No. He's spending the evening with his mother. She's taking his father's death really hard."

"I imagine."

"And since he's their only child, she's leaning on him a lot."

"He's a good son and a good man," Marilyn said. Raven's mother was Carson's biggest fan. Raven had no doubt that her mother was hinting she shouldn't let Donovan ruin her good relationship. Her mother would probably bring it up more directly later.

Raven nodded. "I know."

"I'll make a casserole and a cake and drop it off to-morrow," Marilyn added.

"I'll go with you." She'd spoken to Carson a couple of times since his father's sudden death, but they hadn't spent much time alone. He and his father hadn't been close when Carson was growing up, but they'd grown close over the past few years.

Her father picked up the Remote and turned on the television. It was time for his favorite show and his par-ticipation in the conversation was done. Her mother put on her glasses and picked up her needlepoint, so Raven considered herself dismissed.

The day had been hot and sticky but now that the sun had set, the weather was pleasant. Raven went out to the porch and sat on the wicker love seat, placing her feet on the wooden chest. She inhaled the sweet night air, trying to rid herself of the day's tension.

Letting her head fall against the back of the seat, she closed her eyes and allowed her mind to float free. Usually she spent at least part of the evening replaying the events of the day. Not tonight. Today had been emotionally draining and she didn't want to relive it. Oh, she was happy that Donovan was alive and unhurt. How could she not be? She just wished he'd contacted her years ago if only to tell her that he'd started his life over somewhere else. Without her. That way she wouldn't have wasted ten years of her life waiting for him to come back to her.

Just thinking of her lost years angered her, although she wasn't sure whether she was angrier with Donovan or with herself. Her mother had tried to encourage her to move on, but Raven hadn't been willing to for years. She'd foolishly believed in a love that had only been a mirage. One thing was sure. She was never going to be that stupid again. She'd spend time with Donovan to allow him to establish a relationship with Elias. But there was no way she'd ever let him near her heart again.

Her phone rang and she fished it out of her pocket. One look at the screen and her annoyance flared. Donovan. What could he possibly want? They'd just talked four hours ago. He had gone ten years without speaking to her and now he wouldn't leave her alone. She briefly considered not answering but her curiosity got the better of her. Besides, he lived close enough that he might just pop over.

"Yes?" she answered. *Hello,* no matter how curtly spoken, wouldn't have adequately expressed her irritation.

"Raven?" Donovan's voice was quiet and deeper than this afternoon. Hearing it now brought back memories of the endless hours they'd spent on the telephone while they'd been dating. Though they'd regularly met at their secret place, they hadn't been able to get enough of each other and they'd had intimate phone conversations, as well.

She found herself smiling and forced the reminiscence away. Those nightly conversations had meant everything to her but they'd meant nothing to him. She'd do well to remember that. "Were you expecting someone else? This is my number you called."

He laughed. "True enough. Listen, I hope I'm not bothering you. I was just thinking about things Elias and I can do together."

"Elias, you and me."

"Of course. And you. I would never forget about you, Raven."

She rolled her eyes at how easily the lie slid from his lips. He'd forgotten about her for ten years. "Sure."

"I never forgot about you, Raven," he said as though reading her mind.

"You just never had time to call." She hated how sad she sounded. The last thing she wanted was for him to know how badly he'd hurt her. "Anyway, I'm sure you didn't call to rehash the past. What can I do for you?"

He was silent. For a minute she thought he might explain why he hadn't contacted her, but he didn't. "Elias mentioned a carnival in Sweet Briar. He seemed excited to go, so I thought we could do that. We could have fun and get to know each other gradually."

"Let me think about it, okay?"

"What did you tell him about me?"

"You were there. You heard every word I said. He didn't bring you up again and neither did I."

"I meant about his father. Obviously you didn't tell him my name."

"No. I told him that his father loved him and that he had to go away."

"Anything else?"

"I didn't know anything else," she snapped. "I still don't."

"Raven."

"Never mind. I don't care anymore. It won't change a thing. What we had is past. We've both moved on. I'd prefer not to discuss the past." Nothing could give her back those years. Talking about it would only make her feel more foolish.

"Okay. For now."

"No. Not for now. For always. I mean it. If you want to see Elias, you won't mention the past or give me a bunch of excuses for why you left and didn't have the courtesy to contact me. Bring it up again and you'll have to fight me for visitation. Given your prolonged absence, I don't think any judge will give it to you." She couldn't actually be cruel enough to keep father and son apart, but Donovan didn't know that.

His heavy sigh was his only response.

"I'll let you know about the carnival," she finally said.

"Thank you."

Raven ended the call without saying goodbye. The conversation had unsettled her so she went inside. Perhaps a long soak in the tub would work some magic. If it didn't, she was in for a long, sleepless night.

* * *

Donovan stared at his phone before he put it down. That had gone sideways fast. Raven had actually threatened to keep Elias from him. He didn't know if she'd meant it, but it hadn't been worth pushing her to find out. And really, what difference would it make if she knew the reason he'd left? Nothing would change. They would still have spent the past ten years apart. Their love would still have faded until it no longer existed.

Sure, if she knew the truth she might not hate him, but he knew her heart. She was a kind person and couldn't hold a grudge. If they spent enough time together, they could become friends again. And if the right time came along, he would tell her the truth. But not right now. She was still shaky and trying to figure out things. He was, too. He couldn't say anything now. But maybe when they were both settled and he was sure it wouldn't do more harm than good, he'd tell her about Karl Rivers's threat. In the meantime, he'd have to live with her thinking the worst of him.

Restless, he left his room and went downstairs. His parents were sitting on the rockers on the front porch, the way they always had on nice nights. It was comforting to know that some things hadn't changed. The tragedy of his disappearance and presumed death hadn't torn them apart. They loved each other as much as ever. Now that the threat had been permanently removed and he was no longer in danger, he hoped to find someone to love for a lifetime, too.

Once he'd thought he'd found that with Raven, but he'd been wrong. Their time had passed. Perhaps if he'd lived there for the past ten years, they would have stayed in love. Naturally they'd have gotten married because of the baby. A child deserved both parents. He'd loved Raven and had planned to marry her when they were older, so he wouldn't have minded moving up the date a few years. Maybe they would have had a happy marriage and added a couple more kids. Or maybe they would have grown to resent each other. Who knew? Still, he wished he had had the chance to find out.

But there was no going back and changing things. Ahead was the only way to go. He'd lost ten years of his life already. He wasn't going to waste more time wondering *what if*.

He stepped onto the porch. "I met my son today."

His parents stopped rocking and looked at him. Though the moon was bright and the sky was filled with stars, he couldn't make out the expressions on their faces, so he reached inside the door and switched on the porch light.

"Elias?" His father's voice was soft, filled with guilt.

"Were you going to tell me?"

"Only if Raven didn't."

"What? And how long were you going to wait before you said anything?" He didn't understand how they could keep his son a secret from him.

"We knew you would go see her before long," his mother said. "You weren't here a day before you went over there. Ten years away and nothing has changed. She's still important to you."

That's what she thought. Everything had changed. Of course his mother was a hopeless romantic who thought love could survive anything—including a ten-year absence. It wasn't true, but there was no sense in debating that now.

"Raven took it hard when you left," Mario continued.

"That poor child was a wreck. For a while it looked like we might lose her. When her parents discovered she was pregnant, they told us. To be honest, we weren't in much better shape than Raven was. We supported her decision to keep the baby, but we weren't in a position to provide the emotional support she needed. We were barely holding on ourselves."

"And we were still trying to find you," Lena added. "When the police stopped looking, we put up fliers and did everything we could think of."

"Elias doesn't know you're his grandparents."

"No. We love him and see him now and then. We give him Christmas and birthday presents. He thinks of us as his grandparents' friends."

"And that's enough for you?"

Mario nodded. "You don't realize how bad we were when we couldn't find you. We were a mess. That child didn't need us bringing stress to his life."

Donovan nodded. He understood. Everyone had done the best they could in a difficult situation. He'd suffered a lot when he'd first left home, not knowing if he'd ever return. He'd been young and scared, traveling from place to place, constantly looking over his shoulder. Too cautious to take Karl Rivers at his word, and expecting the man to come after him at any time, it had been years before Donovan had felt comfortable enough to stay in one place. He'd rambled from ranch to ranch, town to town, every few months.

Then he'd met Della and Gabe Turner, owners of an enormous cattle ranch in the middle of Texas. Warm and generous, they treated their ranch hands like family.

After he'd worked on the ranch for a couple of months, Della invited him to have Christmas dinner with her family. He'd turned her down at first, unwilling to get close to anyone. After watching as car after car arrived with people carrying presents, loneliness had gotten the better of him and he'd knocked on her back door. The entire Turner family had welcomed him into the fold. Two of Della and Gabe's sons were near his age and had come home from college for winter break. They'd hit it off. Being around Dustin and Austin had brought back memories of hanging out with Jericho, Tony and Billy.

That day marked a change in Donovan. While other employers had been willing to allow Donovan to keep to himself, the Turners hadn't.

Not that they'd forced him to become a part of their family. They hadn't. Instead they'd seeded the ground with breadcrumbs of kindness. Tired of being alone, he'd followed the trail and found a welcoming family.

With the sons away from the ranch, Donovan had been entrusted with the role of big brother to fifteen-year-old Amelia. As expected, she'd resisted. Once he'd convinced her that he didn't intend to invade her privacy, they'd become friends. He'd often driven her to town to hang out with her friends. If he happened to stick around longer than she would have preferred, well he was okay with that. The Turners had been good to him and he intended to repay them in the best way he knew—by protecting Amelia.

One night he'd actually had to step in when Amelia's date had gotten aggressive, refusing to take no for an answer. When Donovan had seen the way Amelia had tried to hold her torn blouse together, he'd come near to losing control. But Amelia's need for comfort had outweighed his need for revenge.

After that night, he and Amelia had shared a special bond. Their relationship had truly become like siblings. Just as he'd taken his job of protective big brother seriously, she'd taken the role of pesky little sister to heart. She'd decided that he needed a girlfriend and made it her life's mission to find him one. She was constantly introducing him to her friends' female relatives or even women she had just met. Although Donovan had found some of them attractive, he'd guarded his heart, never let any of them get close to him.

Leaving Raven behind had broken him. He would never let himself love that way again. His life had become transitory and his stay on the Turners' ranch while good, was temporary. He wouldn't subject himself or anyone else to the pain that would come when he left. Looking back, he'd been right not to become involved with anyone. He wouldn't be returning to Texas. He had a son and he'd never leave Elias behind.

"I understand. But eventually I want to tell Elias that I'm his father. I intend to be a part of his life."

His parents exchanged a look. "Did Raven say anything else?"

"No. We're still finding our way. Eventually we'll work out everything. When that happens, Elias will know that you're his grandparents. Are you ready for that?"

His mother smiled. "Absolutely."

"Good."

Donovan was finally getting his life and family together. It wasn't the way he'd pictured it years ago, but it still could be good.

Chapter Five

Raven stood beside her fiancé, thanking the many guests who had showed up to pay their respects to Karl Rivers. Raven hadn't known the older man very well—she'd caught him looking at her oddly on more than one occasion and she'd never felt entirely comfortable in his presence—but she felt it was her duty to stand by Carson in his hour of need. He'd been there for her when she'd needed him. Though her parents had supported her during her pregnancy and helped her raise Elias, Carson's friendship had been invaluable.

Carson had been a bit of a nerd in school and despite his father's money and influence, or perhaps because of it, he'd been targeted by bullies. Donovan had taken it upon himself to protect Carson, letting everyone know that if they messed with Carson they would answer to him. He'd never spelled out what would happen if anyone bothered Carson, but he hadn't had to. Donovan had been the most popular kid in school and no one wanted to risk being on the outs with him, so the bullying had stopped.

When Donovan disappeared, Carson began to come around. He'd spent time with her and Elias, being the friend she'd needed. He'd accompanied her whenever she'd chased a lead that she hoped would help her find Donovan, and he'd held her as she'd cried when the information didn't pan out. But most of all he'd been a good, supportive friend. No matter how often she told the story of how she and Donovan fell in love, or the times they'd spent riding or fishing or doing nothing, he listened. He'd never once told her she needed to put the past behind her.

She'd been surprised when he'd gotten her a diamond engagement ring and proposed in front of Elias and her parents last Christmas. Her mother had clapped her hands in delight but her father hadn't said a word. Elias had been too busy studying the titles of his new treasure trove of books to pay much attention to what the adults were doing. Her first thought had been of Donovan and how they'd planned to get married one day. She'd then reminded herself that Donovan was gone and she needed to move on. Who better to do that with than her trusted friend? She wasn't in love with him, but he'd been confident that they'd make each other happy. So she'd said yes.

"I need a break," Carson whispered, pulling her out of her musing.

"Of course." Most of the people had eaten and left already. The last few stragglers probably needed a nudge from the minister to leave.

They wandered outside to the covered patio and walked across the manicured grounds until they found a quiet corner. "I don't understand the need to hang around after a funeral. Didn't it occur to anyone that my mother and I would like some time alone?"

"I think they mean well."

Carson shrugged and blew out a breath. He looked tired and sad. Raven didn't expect that he'd slept much these past few days.

"Where is your mother?"

"She has a headache so she went to her room to lie down. I guess that wasn't a big enough hint."

"They don't mean to be rude. They probably think their presence is comforting to you. If you want, I can get the pastor to make an announcement letting everyone know you appreciate their kindness but that you and your mother want to be alone."

"Maybe later." He stared over her shoulder for so long that she turned and looked. There was no one there.

"Are you okay?"

"I think we should move up the wedding."

"What? Why?"

"It's not like it's going to be a big ceremony."

"True." He'd initially wanted a big wedding and reception but she'd balked. She wanted something simple, just family and very close friends. "But we've already set the date."

"It was just a thought."

He sounded put out but she let it pass. He'd buried his father a few hours ago so she was willing to make a few allowances.

"I heard that Donovan is back in town."

She stiffened. Of course he'd found out. The community was small and word traveled fast. A story this fantastic was bound to make the rounds in double time. Even though they'd never discovered why he'd vanished, everyone had hoped and prayed for his return.

So sure enough, when Donovan had returned alive and well, people had been overjoyed. The love the ranchers and townspeople had for him hadn't faded. Still, with everything that had been going on in Carson's life, she was surprised he'd heard. "Yes. He came back two days ago."

"And you didn't tell me?"

"Your father had just died. I didn't think you would be concerned about Donovan."

"Well, I am."

"I see. Is that why you want to move up our wedding?"

"You never wear your ring."

He didn't answer her question, choosing instead to change the subject, but Raven again let that pass without comment. "I work on a ranch. Do you really want me to wear a diamond ring when I'm working with animals all day?"

"Is that the only reason?"

"Where is all of this coming from?"

"Forget I said anything. I'm just messed up right now. My father is dead and I don't know how to help my mother. She's so sad. She's barely eaten a thing in days."

"She's probably still in shock and trying to process everything. They were married for thirty-five years. He was the love of her life. And now he's gone. She's grieving."

"Just like you did when Donovan disappeared. Is he the love of your life? Or am I?"

"Why are you asking me this now?"

"I notice you didn't answer my question."

Did he want her to lie? She'd never pretended to be in love with him.

"Excuse me."

They spun around and came face-to-face with Sarah Thomas, the pastor's wife. Her face didn't mask her confusion. Clearly she'd heard a good deal of what they'd been saying. Raven knew the good woman would never repeat a word, though.

"I'm sorry to interrupt your conversation, but I want to let you know that everyone has gone. The Mothers Board put the leftovers in the refrigerator and cleaned up the kitchen. Pastor and I want to make sure you or your mother don't need anything before we leave."

"Thank you." Carson put his arm around Mrs. Thomas's shoulder. "I don't know how my mother and I would have managed without your help these past few days."

Although the words were the right ones to say given the situation, Raven had a feeling he was hinting that she hadn't been supportive, which was a crock. She'd been there every minute she could. She was a single mother and her child needed her. Besides, she knew his implied accusation wasn't about anything she had or hadn't done but rather because Carson was upset she hadn't told him Donovan was in town. He was feeling insecure because he knew better than anyone how devastated she'd been these past years. But he only got to use this excuse once.

"I probably should go, too," Raven said after the pastor and his wife drove off.

"That's probably a good idea."

Raven gathered her things and headed to her car. Carson was upset and grieving, so it wasn't the time to have a serious discussion. But they were going to have to talk before their wedding.

Donovan released Zeus into the corral and started across the grass to the house. It had been a long day but a fulfilling one. Being home felt good if a little strange. Having his parents in his life again filled a hole that had been in his soul so long it had become a part of him. The past few days had been exhilarating and better than he had ever imagined they could be. He'd found a son he didn't know he had. That should be enough to keep him happy. But oddly enough it wasn't.

There was a longing inside him for more. He wanted a woman in his life. In the years he'd been away, he'd deliberately held himself aloof. Now he was ready for a relationship. He wanted the kind of love his parents shared. The kind of love that Della and Gabe Turner had.

There was a part of him that missed the Turners. Over the past few years they had been a substitute family for him and he'd come to love them. He felt bad for the way he'd left. It had been almost a week and he hadn't contacted them. If nothing else, he should call to let them know he'd arrived safely and that all was well. And yet there was something holding him back. The very thought of contacting them seemed disloyal to his parents.

It was one thing to love the Turners when he'd had no hope of seeing his mother and father again. But now that he was home, he felt as if all of his love should once more go to his own mom and dad. It didn't make sense, but they'd missed ten years of his life. Surely they deserved to have his time and all of his love. After all, he'd missed nearly the same amount of time with his son. Just thinking that someone else had had the opportunity to watch Elias grow when he'd been denied that privilege was irritating.

When he reached the back patio he saw his mother sitting at a table with someone. It was a minute before he recognized Carson Rivers, but when he did it took all that he had not to react with misplaced anger and snatch the other man by his shirt and throw him off the ranch. He blew out a breath and reminded himself that Carson wasn't to blame for his father's sins.

Carson hadn't been one of his close friends, but Donovan had invited him over from time to time. Lena had always said Carson just needed a little more love and attention than he'd gotten from his parents, so she'd always been especially kind to him. Now, though, Donovan sensed tension between them. No doubt his mother was struggling not to hold Carson responsible for what his father had done to their family.

Donovan reminded himself of the kid Carson had been years ago and smiled. He held out his hand. "Carson. How are you?"

Carson shook Donovan's hand.

Lena jumped from her chair as if anxious to get away. "I'll leave you guys to talk. I've already offered Carson some refreshments, but he didn't want any. Do you want something, Donovan?"

"No thanks, Ma."

Donovan waved Carson back to his chair and they sat as Lena returned to the house. Donovan knew that Carson had buried his father that very morning, but there was no way he could force himself to offer his condolences. No one in the world was as happy as Donovan that Karl Rivers was dead. He only wished the old man had died sooner.

"What brings you around?"

"I heard that you were back in town and wanted to welcome you back."

The tone of voice and the expression on Carson's face were anything but welcoming. Perhaps he sounded so strained because he was trying to keep his grief under control. But why was he here now? It didn't make sense. He could welcome Donovan back anytime. It wasn't as if he was leaving again.

"Thanks." Years spent alone had taught Donovan the waiting game. Carson would get to whatever it was he'd come to say sooner or later.

"A lot has happened since you've been gone."

"True. But a lot has stayed the same. And what changes I've seen have all been positive." Elias being the primary one. That and knowing Karl Rivers was currently rotting in the ground and soon to be devoured by worms.

Carson tapped his finger on the glass table then shifted in his chair. Obviously he had something to say that he didn't think could wait, so why didn't he just spit it out?

"I know you've seen Raven."

Raven? Donovan went on high alert. What did Carson have to do with Raven? "I have."

"And you know about Elias?"

"My son? Yes."

"He's a good kid. And I want you to know that I intend to treat him as if he was my own son."

"What are you talking about?"

"Didn't she tell you?"

"Tell me what?"

"Raven and I are engaged. We're getting married next month. Sooner if I can talk her into it. I'm planning on adopting Elias."

"The hell you are."

Rage filled Donovan. Karl Rivers had stolen ten years of his life. There was no way he was going to allow Karl Rivers's son to step into the role that was supposed to be his. "I don't know what you and Raven have planned. If you get married, that's between the two of you. But as far as my son goes, I'm his father. He's not going to need you to treat him like a son. And I will never consent to letting him be adopted, so you can just file that under things that will never happen in this lifetime."

"You think you can just waltz back here after ten years and take up where you left off?"

"What I think is none of your damn business."

"You left. Raven has moved on. With me. I have no intention of stepping aside because you've decided that you want to live in Sweet Briar after all."

Donovan jumped to his feet and Carson stood, as well. They were about the same height and build, but Donovan had no doubt, as furious as he was, he could demolish the other man in under sixty seconds. "I never wanted to leave Sweet Briar. If not for your bastard of a father, I would have been here to watch my son be born. I would have been with him every day. I missed the first half of his life, but there is no way I'm going to stand back and let you steal the rest. I'll see you in hell first. I suggest you get off my property while you can still walk."

"Wait. What?" Carson's eyes widened and his voice shook. He looked like he'd seen a ghost. "What do you mean if not for my father you wouldn't have left Sweet Briar? He put up money to try to find you."

"Your dear old dad threatened to kill me. And my family. And Raven."

Donovan had been concerned about Raven's reaction and hadn't wanted her to know about the threat. But she was engaged to Carson and her health was no longer Donovan's concern. Let her fiancé take care of her. Donovan was through trying to protect someone who was keeping secrets from him.

"I don't believe it. You'd say anything to get Raven back."

Even though Carson said the words, Donovan heard the lack of conviction in his voice. Carson had his doubts. Had he seen or heard something over the years that made him suspicious? Donovan didn't care. The only thing that mattered was Elias.

"I'm not interested in getting Raven back. As you pointed out, ten years have passed. I don't love her anymore, so I have no reason to lie. Your father threatened us. I don't care if you don't believe me. Now, for the last time, get off my property. And don't come back."

Donovan told himself to calm down as he watched the other man stumble across the patio and to his truck. No doubt Carson had been blindsided by the truth of who his father really was. Was it possible he hadn't had a clue? Maybe. And the part of Donovan that had liked Carson as a teenager felt bad for causing the other man more grief on what for him had to be a sad day, but he brushed aside the sentiment.

Carson had come there intent on staking his claim by letting Donovan know Raven was engaged. Carson hadn't cared about Donovan's feelings, so if Carson left with a little more knowledge than what he came with? Too bad. Life was rough.

Donovan exhaled, trying to breathe out the bitterness. Still he acknowledged that the other man had hit his mark. Carson was walking away with the one woman Donovan had loved.

Raven was getting married.

Chapter Six

"Why don't you go help Granddad?"

"Okay, but we're still going, right?" Elias asked for the umpteenth time. Raven always tried to keep her word, so his need for reassurance only emphasized how much going to the carnival meant to him.

"Yes. But we don't need to leave for a couple of hours. You might as well do something constructive instead of watching the clock." And driving her crazy. Goodness knows there were enough things going on in her life to wreck her nerves without Elias following her around as she cleaned the house.

"Okay." He set the alarm on his phone and opened the back door. "I'll be back in exactly two hours."

The door slammed behind him and Raven let out a deep sigh that did nothing to relieve her stress. She had agreed to let Donovan join her and Elias at the carnival. Donovan had wanted to drive to Sweet Briar with them, but she'd turned him down flat. This wasn't a date. Besides, going together would raise too many questions that she wasn't equipped to answer right now. Elias knew that she and Carson planned to get married in a few weeks. At his age he might not understand the finer nuances of relationships, but he knew an engaged woman wasn't supposed to go out with other men. To be honest, Carson wasn't too pleased about it either—in fact they'd had a big argument over her decision—but she had to do what was best for her son.

She'd convinced Donovan to "accidently" bump into them in town. Then she would invite him to walk around with them. That shouldn't raise too much suspicion. At least not with Elias. Raven was certain that several eyebrows would rise at the sight of her and Donovan together. Without a doubt, tongues would be wagging before the sun went down. Though she knew the talk wouldn't be vicious—for the most part people in Sweet Briar and the surrounding area were kind—Raven didn't relish being the topic that kept the phone lines burning for the next few weeks.

But the truth was, whether or not she and Donovan were spotted riding the bumper cars together—something she had no intention of doing—they were going to be the subject of gossip. Donovan was bound to be the main topic of conversation for the foreseeable future. It wasn't every day that someone who had been missing and presumed dead returned to town alive and well. Add in the mysterious way he'd vanished and the question of where he'd been all this time and this was a story worth telling over and over again. And since they'd been dating at the time of his disappearance, her name was likely to come up.

As far as she knew, Donovan hadn't been to town yet so he was bound to be as big as attraction as the carnival itself.

"I think you're making a mistake."

Raven hadn't heard her mother's approach, so at the sound of Marilyn's voice, she jumped. Raven didn't pretend not to know what her mother was talking about. "You're entitled to your opinion."

Marilyn put her hand on her hip. "Raven."

"Donovan is Elias's father. He has a right to get to know his son."

"He gave up that right when he left you alone and pregnant."

Raven blew out an irritated breath. Not that again. Her mother had been singing that same old song since Raven had told her Donovan was back. "He didn't know about the baby. I didn't get a chance to tell him."

Marilyn waved her hand, clearly dismissing Raven's words as if they were of no value. Raven loved her mother and appreciated everything she'd done to help with Elias, but *she* was Elias's mother. And as his mother, she was tasked with making decisions on his behalf.

"And what about Carson? I'm sure your fiancé can't be excited about having Donovan sniffing around you again."

"He's not 'sniffing around' me as you call it. The only thing he wants is to get to know his son."

"And Carson?"

Raven frowned. "He's not exactly pleased by the

situation. But he's going to have to adjust, just like the rest of us. Donovan isn't going anywhere."

"I wouldn't be so sure of that. That boy is unreliable."

"First of all, he's no longer a boy. He's a man. And you used to adore him."

"That was before he broke your heart and left you all alone, barely able to make it through the day. And look at what he did to Lena and Mario. The grief he put them through for years. So, no, I have no use for him. Now Carson? That man is steady. He's faithful. He won't let you down."

"And that should be enough for me? The fact that I can depend on him should be enough to base a marriage on?" Raven didn't know where the doubts were coming from but they were coming fast and hard. Or maybe they'd been lurking below the surface all along and were pushing to the top.

"It doesn't hurt. You were so sure about Carson before. Donovan hasn't been in town long enough to unpack and you're questioning your relationship with a good man. Don't be foolish, Raven. Don't throw away a solid relationship because of what you imagine you can have with Donovan. Life isn't a fairy tale. I know he's Elias's biological father, but he's not good for you. He doesn't love you. He'll break your heart again sure as you're standing here, if you give him a chance. Don't let him. Stay with the good man."

"What about love?"

"What about it? You loved Carson five months ago when you accepted his marriage proposal. You're just confused because Donovan is back in town and you're swept away by the romance of it all. Trust me, whatever you're feeling isn't love. And I don't believe Donovan will stick around. It's better to bet on the sure thing instead of risking it all and ending up with nothing."

"Is that what you did?" Raven knew the answer to that question. Her parents had been a love match. Marilyn's parents hadn't approved of Rudy because they'd thought he was too old for her. They'd also wanted her to go to college before she married. So Rudy and Marilyn had eloped the day after she'd graduated from high school. Raven's grandparents had been furious and disappointed. That disappointment had disappeared when Marilyn started college the following fall. They'd been beyond proud when she'd graduated at the top of her class four years later.

Her mother had the good grace to look flustered. "No. But our situations are different."

"Because I'm a single mother?"

"Of course not."

"Then why?"

Marilyn chuckled. "Because you're my little girl and I don't want you to get hurt again."

"I want what you and Dad have. I want a love so strong that it lights up a room. A love that people can see from miles away."

"You can have that with Carson."

"I'm not sure."

"You don't think you have that with Donovan." Marilyn sounded aghast at the very notion.

"I don't know. We haven't seen each other in years. I don't even know him. Not really."

"Well, I wouldn't be so willing to throw away what you can have with Carson on a man you barely know now."

Having had the last word, Marilyn walked away.

Raven hadn't expected her mother to change her position on Carson easily and she hadn't. Her father was the romantic parent. He'd tell her to follow her heart wherever it led. Regardless of whose direction she followed, Raven was left with the problem of facing Donovan again.

Because, ready or not, in a little over an hour she and Elias would be on their way to "accidently" meeting him.

Donovan stood in the shadow of the building near the entrance to the carnival and watched as the crowd grew. He'd deliberately arrived early because he'd wanted to get the lay of the land. He'd parked near city hall and walked around town for about an hour. Sweet Briar, a small beach town, had grown significantly in the years he'd been gone and, from all appearances, was thriving. New businesses had popped up and the older ones looked more prosperous than he'd remembered.

Driving to town, he'd been surprised to see a couple of subdivisions of huge houses on what had previously been open land. The narrow and bumpy road he remembered had been widened and paved.

As he'd neared the spot that had been indelibly marked on his mind, his stomach had clenched and his palms had become sweaty. He'd pressed down on the accelerator, anxious to speed by the place where his life had been so drastically changed.

It looked no different from any other stretch of the road. Passing, he felt…nothing. Not fear. Not anger. Nothing. The trepidation dissipated and he'd continued on to Sweet Briar and the carnival.

Growing up on a ranch, coming to town for a reason

other than to attend school had been a big deal. Mabel's Diner had been the Friday-night hangout for all of the teenagers. He and his friends had spent countless hours there. He grinned as he recalled gobbling down burgers, shakes and fries mere hours after eating a big dinner with his parents. The diner had been open for business when he'd passed it earlier, but he hadn't stepped inside. He had peered through the plate-glass window and was pleased to note that the interior hadn't changed. The same red-vinyl booths lined the walls. He wouldn't be surprised if the menu was the same.

After his stroll through the town, he'd come to where he now stood. He checked his watch. Raven and Elias weren't due for another ten minutes. He could walk around some more but he didn't want to miss them.

"Donovan?"

He turned and watched a man and woman approaching. As they neared, Donovan smiled. "Jericho."

Laughing, they pounded each other on the back as they embraced.

"It's good to see you. I heard that you were back in town but I needed to see for myself before I could believe it." Jericho Jones laughed and shook his head. "Even though I'm staring right at you, I can't believe you're really here. We looked all over for you, but it was like you'd vanished into thin air. Where were you all this time?"

"Texas. At least for the past seven years." It was clear Jericho wanted more of an answer than that, but that was the best Donovan could do right now. He didn't want to pollute the night with talk of Karl Rivers. Later he would tell his old friend the whole story without leaving out a single detail. But not now.

"Why didn't you come back or call? Something?" Jericho sounded confused and frustrated.

Coming home was definitely more difficult than Donovan had anticipated. As he searched for words, the woman beside Jericho cleared her throat loudly. Thank goodness.

"Sorry. Let me introduce you to my wife, Camille."

She extended a hand, which Donovan shook. "Nice to meet you, Camille."

"You, too. I've heard so much about you, I feel like I already know you. Don't let the curious people press you for more information than you're comfortable giving. I had to get out of town rather quickly myself once, so I understand. Lucky for me, I ran to this rancher who saved me." She and Jericho smiled at each other. The love between them was apparent and Donovan's heart ached with longing.

Jericho laughed and gently squeezed his wife's shoulder before looking at Donovan again. "Camille is right. I apologize for being nosy. I'm just glad you're home again. You're staying, right?"

"Yes. The ranch is my home." And the life and people he'd left behind in Texas? Where did they fit? He'd figure that out later. Right now building a relationship with his son took priority over everything. Donovan looked at Camille. "Maybe I'm as nosy as Jericho because I'm curious about what you meant by getting out of town quickly. But don't tell me if you don't want to."

She smiled. "No worries. Before becoming a rancher's wife I was a city girl. New York City, to be exact. I discovered money laundering in my Wall Street job and reported it. A little while later I overheard my boss plotting to kill me. I didn't waste time. I beat it out of New York and raced to the Double J. This heroic rancher took me in. We fell in love and the rest, as they say, is history."

"Wow." Her story didn't sound all that different from his and he found comfort and hope in that. Despite everything she'd endured, she'd fallen in love and was happily married. Maybe he could have a happy ending, too.

"Yes. So you see, no matter what your story is, it won't seem too farfetched for us."

"I'll keep that in mind." Donovan rubbed the back of his neck. "Do Billy and Tony still live around here? I would love to catch up with them."

Jericho shook his head. "You remember Tony went to UCLA, right?"

"Yes. He'd been blue and gold all the way."

"He stayed in California after college. His parents retired to Hilton Head about five years ago. Their ranch had originally been part of the Double J, so I bought it. When he comes back to visit them, he stops in for a day or two, but that's about it."

"And Billy?"

A look of sorrow crossed Jericho's face. "He was killed in Iraq eight years ago."

"Oh, man."

"Yeah. His parents and sisters are still around, though I don't see them all that much. To be honest, I'd lost touch with people myself for a while there. I've been trying to do a better job of keeping in touch with my friends, so consider this an open invitation to come out to the ranch anytime you want."

"And hang out in the clubhouse?"

Jericho laughed. "Nah. I'm afraid the clubhouse has

been torn down. You'll have to settle for sitting on the patio."

"Will do. I'll drop by sometime next week."

Jericho nodded. "Do that. We're going to get a couple of funnel cakes. Do you want to join us?"

Donovan shook his head. "I'll catch up with you later."

Donovan watched as Jericho and Camille meandered through the crowd. It was good to see his old friend so happy. Maybe he'd be as lucky as Jericho had been and he'd find someone to love, too. He'd think about that later. Right now it was time to meet up with Raven and Elias.

Donovan spotted them as they walked through the entrance and went to the ticket booth. Raven glanced around as she dug through her purse, probably trying to find him without being too obvious.

He took a moment to look at her. Dressed in a pink top and shorts with flowers on them, she was the most beautiful thing he'd ever seen. She packed a lot of sex appeal into her five feet and three inches. She turned away from him, treating him to a perfect view of her straight back, tiny waist and round bottom. Her calves were strong, proof that she not only lived on a ranch, she worked there.

"Come on, Mom," Elias said, reaching out and grabbing Raven by the hand and pulling her after him.

"Okay." She took another look around.

It was time to stop lurking and put the plan into action. Donovan took a deep breath and stepped from the shadows. "Raven? Elias? I thought that was you." He managed to inject his voice with just the right amount of surprise so anyone witnessing the interaction would never suspect that this was a planned meeting. He trotted a little to catch up with them.

"Hi," Raven said. She brushed a lock of hair behind her ear. A small diamond sparkled in her lobe.

"Hey," Elias added. He glanced over his shoulder and took a step toward the rides. Clearly he wasn't interested in making small talk when there was fun to be had.

"I'm here alone. Do you guys mind if I hang out with you?"

"Sure," Raven said. "That should be all right, don't you think, Elias?"

"Uh. Sure. I guess. But you said I could hang out with my friends some, too."

"You can. We'll be behind you."

"But not with us, right? You know I'm nine. That's halfway to being a man. I can take care of myself."

"I know."

Donovan bit back a sigh and a laugh at the same time. Spending time with his son wasn't going to be as easy as he'd hoped. Donovan had envisioned them going from tent to tent together as they played the various games, then sitting side by side on the rides. Instead he was going to be relegated to watching his son do those things from a distance. Still, it was easy to recall feeling the same way when he'd been that age. The last thing he'd wanted was to have his mom and dad close enough to overhear what he and his friends were saying to each other. And God forbid one of his parents make a comment.

"Don't worry. You'll still get plenty of time with him," Raven said as Elias ran off to join a group of five or six boys who then darted to a tent and handed over game tickets.

"You're being nicer about this than I'd expected you to be."

"What did you think I'd do? Grab my kid and go sneaking off in the middle of the night?"

Donovan inhaled a sharp breath.

"Sorry. I didn't mean that the way it sounded."

"I suppose not. I'm just a bit sensitive, I guess."

"And I'm a bit uncomfortable. Have you noticed how many people are staring at us?"

On his walk through town, he had encountered several people he'd recognized. To a person, they'd welcomed him home with a kind word and a smile. "They're not staring at us. They're staring at you. You're the prettiest girl here and they can't help but look."

Raven laughed. "There's no need for flattery. I already said you can spend time with Elias."

"It's not flattery. It's the truth. You're gorgeous."

The laughter vanished from her voice and the sparkle left her eyes. "No flirting. We're not on a date getting to know each other. We're here for Elias."

"But we are getting to know each other. Not for the purpose of falling in love again. I know you're engaged and I respect that."

"Who told you I was engaged?"

"Carson. He stopped by and told me. Congratulations, by the way. I hope you'll be happy together. Just so you know, I have no intention of interfering in your life. But if we're going to co-parent Elias, we need to find a way to be friends again. And we were friends, weren't we?"

She nodded and the smile reappeared. Apparently he'd said the right thing. She poked him in the chest.

"Until you decided that you didn't want to be my friend anymore. You with your boys only club."

"Blame it on Jericho. The club was his idea."

"So you're going to throw your friend under the bus like that."

"Yep. Especially since he's not around to hear me."

Raven laughed again. The sound touched the place in his heart that had once belonged to her.

"I saw him earlier and met his wife."

"Camille? She's great. I'm so glad she came along and got him to live again. He'd become a real recluse. Not that I'm one to talk."

"Jericho Jones? He was always the life of the party."

"That was before his first wife died in childbirth. The baby died, too. After that he shut himself off from everyone. He barely left the Double J and he made it clear he didn't want people coming to see him."

"Wow. I didn't know that."

"You weren't here."

"I know." During the years in Texas, Donovan had always pictured everyone he knew living happy lives. He'd believed he was the only one whose life had been derailed and whose dreams had been shattered. He'd been wrong. Jericho had suffered actual tragedy, losing a wife and child. And Billy had been killed. Learning that shone a different light on his experience. It didn't diminish his pain or right the wrong that had been done to him. Nothing could do that. It simply let him know that life had been hard on others, too.

He looked at Raven. Though her eyes were clear, he knew she'd experienced her share of pain. She'd told him about it that first day. He'd listened but he hadn't really heard. She'd loved him as desperately as he'd loved her. And then she'd lost him just as he'd lost her. But he'd had the benefit of knowing why he'd left so suddenly. She'd had to deal with the unknown. The questions. The heartbreak of unfulfilled yet undying hope. She'd had to worry every day, not knowing if he was dead or alive. For all she'd known he could have been abducted by a serial killer. Or a sadist who'd hurt him for years. The not knowing must have been nerve-racking.

Donovan stepped in front of Raven and took her hands in his. Though she worked on the ranch, her palms were soft. "I'm sorry."

"Sorry for what?"

"For putting you through ten years of hell. Ten years of hoping I'd come home. For not being around while you were pregnant or to help you raise our son. All of it. I'm sorry for all of it. Please forgive me."

Her eyes widened in surprise and she blinked. Was what he'd said so unexpected? He didn't think so. Just what kind of jerk did she think he'd become? He replayed the conversation they'd had that first night. It must have looked like he was playing games when he hadn't fully answered her questions. He could tell her about Karl Rivers now but he didn't want to risk upsetting her. He didn't want to find out if she'd actually follow through on her threat if he mentioned the past. Elias was too important to risk. He didn't want to end up in court fighting for the right to see his son. Besides, Raven was engaged to another man, so his reasons for staying away really didn't matter now. They'd have to start here to build their relationship.

"You're forgiven."

"Clean slate?"

She smiled. "Clean slate. Now let's catch up to Elias and play some games. I plan on winning one of those oversize teddy bears."

As they walked across the field, Donovan felt truly happy. He didn't kid himself that the rough patch between him and Raven was in the past. There were too many unresolved issues for that to be the case. But right now he'd take the temporary peace.

Chapter Seven

Raven took aim with the air rifle and pulled the trigger, knocking over the last moving duck. Raising her hands above her head, she let out a triumphant squeal. "I did it. I won!"

"Yes, you did," Donovan said. "Congratulations."

What had started as a friendly competition between a few parents had turned into a serious battle that had drawn quite a crowd. In the end, Raven was the last person standing.

"I guess all those hunting trips with Dad and my brothers paid off." Rudy had insisted that all of the kids, including Raven, accompany him. To this day Raven suspected her mother had been behind the tradition, using the hunting and fishing trips as a way to have a quiet weekend without her five boisterous kids.

"You won, Mom. You're the only person who shot all the ducks, so you get a big prize and not just one of those plastic rings or necklaces." Despite the fact that his friends were around, Elias gave her a tight hug. His pride touched her heart and she basked in the moment. "Pick your prize. Mom. You can choose between the big rabbit and the pony."

"I want the teddy bear."

"But you already have a big teddy bear at home," Elias pointed out as if she didn't see it every morning. It sat in a rocking chair by the window in her bedroom, so she couldn't miss it.

"I know. This one will be its friend so it won't be lonely."

"They're not alive, Mom. They're toys. They don't have feelings."

She shook her head. Elias had no problem suspending reality when it came to superheroes. But when it came to the whimsical? He became very literal-minded. "You never know."

"But—"

Elias was about to launch into a long, logical argument but Donovan put a hand on his shoulder, stopping him. "Never argue with a woman. You won't come close to winning. If she wants to believe her stuffed toys have feelings, you should just nod and agree."

"But she's wrong."

Donovan winked at Elias. "It makes her feel better to believe it. Okay?"

"Whatever." Elias shrugged. "Can I go with my friends? We want to ride the bumper cars."

Raven nodded. "Be nice and be careful."

"I will." Elias and the other boys raced away, leaving Raven alone with Donovan.

She took the teddy bear from the young man running the game and hugged it close to her chest. When she looked up, Donovan was watching her. "What?"

"You still have that bear I gave you?"

"Yes." They'd gone to an amusement park in Charlotte and he'd won it for her by tossing rings onto empty soda bottles. He'd spent over twenty dollars on tickets before he'd won, but she'd wanted the bear and he'd been determined that she have it. When Donovan had driven her home, he'd told her the bear would watch out for her while she slept and remind her that he would always love her. That bear had been one of the few links she'd had to him these past years and she could not imagine parting with it.

He nodded as if satisfied with her answer. "I can carry your prize if you want."

"And have everyone think you won it?"

"You don't have to worry about that. There's not a person in this place who didn't hear your victory cry. And I'm sure Elias has bragged to anyone who missed it."

"In that case, be my guest." She handed off the stuffed animal and they walked toward the area filled with rides. As they neared, the music of the carousel grew louder. Children carrying half-eaten cotton candy with ice cream stains on their shirts darted from place to place, high on sugar. Their haggard-looking parents trailed after them.

"This has been fun," Donovan said.

"Yes it has." She'd been worried about how it would feel to be around him again, but surprisingly she'd been comfortable. It was like old times minus the hand-holding and stolen kisses. She wasn't going to let down her guard and give him free access to her heart again, but she was willing to put aside her anger and try to become friends for Elias's sake. And though Donovan didn't know the woman she had become over the past decade any more than she knew the man he'd become, they had been good friends as kids even before they'd fallen in love. They'd had a solid basis for rekindling that friendship.

They reached the bumper cars and watched Elias and his friends crash into each other, laughing with glee every time. When the ride was over, Elias walked over to them, his feet dragging. "Kenny's mom and dad said it's getting late and he has to go home."

"I was thinking the same thing," Raven said.

Donovan and Elias groaned simultaneously and then laughed together. And to think she'd worried about how the two of them would get along. She shouldn't have wasted her time. They got on like a house afire. After a few cautious attempts at conversation, Elias and Donovan had discovered a mutual love of comic books. As they'd munched on corn dogs and walking tacos, they'd rated the various superheroes.

"How about one more ride before we go?" Donovan asked. Elias pleaded with his eyes for her to say yes.

"Fine. One ride."

Donovan and Elias looked at each other. "The roller coaster."

"I'll sit this one out," Raven said. She'd been shaken and rattled enough for one day.

As they walked the short distance to the ride, Donovan and Elias picked up their conversation about superheroes.

"If you could have any superpower, even if it's not

one that real superheroes have, which one would you want?" Elias asked.

"I'm not sure. Let me think on it for a minute. Which one would you want?"

"I would want to be invisible," Elias said promptly. "I could go everywhere I wanted to go and nobody would see me."

"That's true. But people might step on your foot and bump into you. That wouldn't be good."

"I could still see them, so I would get out of the way. Plus when it was time to do chores or math homework I would disappear so Mom couldn't see me."

Donovan laughed and Raven shook her head.

"And at night I could read as long as I wanted and Mom wouldn't be able to tell."

"Sure she would."

"How? I'd be invisible. She wouldn't be able to see me."

"Maybe you'd be invisible, but the book wouldn't be. Your mom would see a book floating in the air and the pages turning."

"Yeah. I forgot about that." Elias kicked at some gravel in the road. "So what power would you want, Donovan?"

"Time travel."

"You mean like see the future? That would be good. I could use that to know the problems that my teacher was putting on my math test ahead of time. That way I could get an A."

"Or you could study," Raven added dryly.

Elias rolled his eyes at the very idea. Apparently the notion was too ridiculous to warrant a comment.

"I wouldn't use the power so much to see the future. I'm good with being surprised about what might happen. I would use the power to go back in time and change the past. I would do things differently and avoid some problems. I wouldn't go to the places I'd gone to or see the things I'd seen." Donovan sounded so somber that Raven knew he wasn't just making silly conversation to entertain Elias. He was serious. And she wondered just what he'd seen that he wished he hadn't. Did it have anything to do with why he'd disappeared so abruptly and stayed away so long?

"But if you change the past, then now would be different," Elias said.

"I know. I'm good with that."

"But what if you weren't around somewhere that you should have been? What if you saved somebody in the past? If you weren't there, that person might have been hurt."

Like Amelia. She'd needed him that night. If he hadn't been there, her life would be different. She might not be the vibrant woman she'd become. "I hadn't thought of that. Maybe it's a good thing we don't have superpowers."

"Well, it's a good thing you can't go back in time and mess up things. It still would be great for me to be able to be invisible."

Raven and Donovan looked at each other and laughed. They'd reached the front of the line for the roller coaster so Donovan gave her back the bear. He and Elias boarded, strapped in and pulled the metal bar over their thighs. After all the cars were loaded, the ride started to move and riders cheered in anticipation.

Raven stepped back and sat on a bench to wait, enjoying the minute to sit and people watch. She waved to a couple of folks she'd gone to school with and let some little kids pat her teddy bear. Five minutes later Donovan and Elias returned and they wandered to the parking lot. All in all, it had been a good outing. If things went this smoothly every day, co-parenting was going to be a breeze.

They reached her car first. Elias said goodbye to Donovan then hopped inside. Donovan placed the teddy bear in the back seat and then leaned against the driver's door. "I had a nice time. Thanks for letting me hang with you."

She nodded. Suddenly this felt like the end of a date and she was unsure what to do. Donovan solved that problem by moving out of her way and opening the door for her. He held it as she got inside and then closed it firmly. As she drove away she looked in the rearview mirror. He stood there alone, watching them leave.

Would he be happy to stay on the outside or would he try to shoehorn himself into their lives? And just how far was she willing to let him in?

Donovan stared at the phone for a long moment before he set it on the patio table. That was unexpected. Yesterday things had gone so well with Raven that he'd called and asked for pictures of Elias. He couldn't get back the years of Elias's life that he'd missed, but if he could somehow experience them in pictures, that would take away some of the sting. He didn't see the harm but apparently he'd overstepped. Raven had shot him down, telling him that if he'd wanted to see Elias grow up, he should have stuck around. Then she'd hung up the phone before he could say another word.

Of course, there was nothing he could have said to that anyway.

"Trouble?"

Donovan looked up. He hadn't noticed his parents' approach. "Not really." He didn't want his parents worrying about him. They still watched him more closely than they had when he'd been sixteen. Their fear was as understandable as it was frustrating.

"How was the carnival?" Lena asked as she settled into a chair. The early afternoon sun provided sunlight without excess heat and the cool breeze was the perfect touch to a great day. He'd missed these pleasant days when he'd been in Texas. Now he cherished every moment he spent in the North Carolina weather.

"It was fun."

"I'm glad you and Raven are getting along. I always liked her." Lena sighed. "The two of you made such a cute couple."

He could see where his mother was going with this and stopped her in her tracks. "We were kids then. A lot of water has gone under that bridge. She's engaged to Carson Rivers. There's no going back for us, so don't start trying to turn my life into one of those romantic movies you're always watching."

"Carson's a nice man but he's not right for her. Now that you're back you can help her see that."

"Lena. Leave the boy alone. He can find a girl on his own."

"I'm sure he can. All I did was remind him of how well they'd always gotten along. And they do have a son."

"Lena."

"Okay. I won't say another word about Raven. I'm

sure he remembers how sweet she is. And he'd have to be blind not to see how pretty she is."

Donovan and his father exchanged glances. Clearly his mother was not going to be deterred. She was going to point out all of Raven's virtues one way or the other. Not that he'd missed them. But since she was getting married soon, they just didn't matter.

Mario stood and held out his hand. "Come on, Lena. It's time for our walk."

Lena smiled and took her husband's hand. For as long as Donovan could recall, his parents had taken long walks around the ranch every Sunday afternoon, weather permitting. His father had told him once that carving out special time for the two of them was the glue that held their marriage together. That and communication.

Listening to his parents' voices as they walked away, Donovan wondered if he was making a mistake by not calling Raven back. They would never get anywhere if they didn't communicate. Not that he expected them to restart their romance. She was in love with another man and he was still adjusting to this life and trying to find a way to put the one he'd left behind in Texas behind him.

No matter how happy he was to be home, he missed Texas and the friends who'd become like family.

Della and Gabe Turner had become surrogate parents, their children his siblings. Not that he would ever say that out loud. The words would hurt his parents. He'd already caused them enough pain. He'd have to figure out this problem on his own.

Chapter Eight

Raven twisted the sponge as if she were wringing out the devil before slamming it on the sink. She blew out an exasperated breath. She knew she was sending Donovan mixed signals but she couldn't control the anger that reared its ugly head at unexpected times. One minute she was happy to be with him and the next she was recalling how much time she'd lost because of him and she'd become short-tempered and mean.

After the great time she'd had with him at the carnival, she'd actually believed she was over her anger. She'd been deluding herself. She was furious over the pain she'd endured the past ten years. The enjoyment that she'd missed. The friends she'd lost touch with because she couldn't think of anything except him. Although none of it was his fault—he wasn't responsible for her actions—he could have prevented it. All he'd had to do was let her know he was alive and well and she could have moved on. That he hadn't done so infuriated her and filled her with resentment.

And he'd had the nerve to ask for pictures of Elias. If he'd been around he could have taken pictures himself. He could have been *in* some pictures. And he wanted to have copies of hers? Not in this lifetime.

"Want to talk about it or do you want to torture that poor sponge some more?" Raven's father's amused voice startled her.

She must have looked a sight, mumbling to herself and throwing things. She turned around, intending to tell him no. The concerned look on his face made her change her mind. She didn't have to hide her feelings from her father. He would listen without judgment or criticism. Unlike her mother, he didn't claim to know what was best for her. If she asked for advice, he would offer it. If not, he would kiss her cheek and tell her the answer was within her. She only needed to trust herself.

She pulled out a chair and sat. "I'm angry. I know it's irrational and I shouldn't be, but there it is."

"Why shouldn't you be?" Rudy, asked, sitting across from her. "You feel what you feel. Let's start from there and see where we end up."

"It's Donovan. He wants pictures of Elias."

"And you don't want to give them to him?"

"No."

"Why not?"

"Why should I? He doesn't deserve them. If he wanted to see Elias grow up, he should have been here."

"And he wasn't and you don't know why. So you imagine him living it up while life passed you by."

She nodded.

"Did you ask him why he left?"

"That first day. All he would tell me was that he'd been living in Texas. For all I know he has a wife and ten other kids."

Rudy looked at her as if she'd said something revealing. Had she? Did he think she cared about what Donovan had done with other women? She didn't care if he had five wives and a hundred kids.

Finally her father spoke. "I doubt that seriously. And so do you. And, to be honest, I don't think Donovan is the only one you're upset with."

Sometimes it was hard to believe her father was a rancher and not a psychiatrist. "No. I loved him so much. I thought I was going to die without him. I wanted to. I was so worried that something terrible was happening to him when all along he was going about his life without a care in the world. You and Mom kept telling me to move on, but I didn't. I was a fool. I wasted ten years of my life wishing on stars. And now Donovan wants to see what he missed of Elias's life. I don't get a second chance to relive my life and see what I missed, so why should he?"

"Do you think if you give him the pictures he'll be able to change the past? Looking at the pictures won't suddenly make him a part of Elias's life or give him back all the years he missed. At best, looking at the pictures will be bittersweet for him."

Raven nodded. "I know."

"What else is wrong?"

She closed her eyes. "Having Donovan back in town is making me doubt everything. I'm engaged to Carson, but Donovan wants to get to know Elias. It would be easy to tell him no, but that wouldn't be fair to him or Elias."

"What does Donovan getting to know Elias have to do with your relationship with Carson? The two things seem separate to me."

"It's hard to separate Donovan from the rest of my life. He's not going anywhere. Everything is more complicated with him around."

"Why?"

"Because… I don't know." She slapped her hand on the table. "Everything was clear before he came back. I'm not saying he shouldn't have come back. That would be a horrible thing to even think. It just would have been easier if he'd come home after the wedding."

"Maybe. Or maybe it would have been worse. It's understandable that you're feeling confused right now. You and Donovan left a lot of things unfinished. When he left, you were still very much in love with him. You carried that love and hope inside you for ten years. You bore his child. Now that he's back, those feelings are resurfacing along with anger and confusion. The question you have to ask yourself is whether that love is still there. And if it is, is it strong enough to survive in the present with all of its complications."

"I'm so confused. I'm not sure marrying Carson is the right thing to do anymore. And that only makes me angrier at Donovan. It's all his fault."

"Is it?"

"What do you mean?"

"He's not responsible for you holding on to him for all these years. That was your choice."

"I just knew in my heart that he wasn't dead. I believed that one day he would come back to me."

"And when he did, he didn't have a good explanation for why he'd left you and you'd promised another man that you'd marry him."

"Yes. It's all a big mess. Nothing is clear anymore. I don't know what to do."

"Do the right thing."

She buried her face in her hands. "And what would that be?"

"That's something that only you know. You just need to listen to that voice inside. You might not see the entire picture now, but you don't need to. Don't worry about what might happen a year from now. Focus on today. Just consider what the right thing is for the issue you're facing now—the pictures—and do that. One step at a time. Remember—"

"I know. The answer is in me."

"That's my girl." He kissed her forehead and then left.

Raven sat for a minute, trying to sort out her thoughts. She had no idea what the right thing would be in the future, but she knew the right thing to do now. She went to her room where she kept most of Elias's pictures. She had a thick volume for each year of his life. Today she'd give Donovan one or two pictures from each book. Doing the right thing was a process and this was the best she could do today.

After she'd chosen her favorites, she stuck the pictures in a manila envelope. Elias was spending the day with his best friend, Kenny, so there was no reason she couldn't drop the pictures off right now. She went downstairs before she could change her mind. Her father was going through ranch books in the kitchen. She held up the envelope.

"I take it you reached a decision."

"Yep. I'm going to drop them off before I talk myself out of it."

"That's the spirit."

Knowing she was doing the right thing made her feel better and she hummed a little tune as she grabbed the truck keys and headed for the Cordero ranch.

Donovan heard a car approaching and opened his eyes. His parents were still strolling—they had been known to be gone for hours—so it was up to Donovan to welcome the visitor. He got to the front door and went out just in time to see a Mercedes SUV pull into the driveway. Carson emerged from the vehicle before it had come to a complete stop. He was holding a leather-bound book in one hand and a few sheets of paper in the other.

"What did you see?" Carson yelled as he neared Donovan.

"What are you talking about?"

"Don't play dumb with me. The other day you hinted that my father was the reason you left. I found his journals. Not the ones he wrote for posterity's sake, just in case someone wanted to write a biography about what a great man he was. No. I found the one he hid. The one he died before he had a chance to destroy."

Carson swung the book wildly and Donovan ducked to avoid being hit. It was evident that Carson had discovered his father wasn't who he'd believed him to be and was taking it hard. Donovan felt for the other man. It couldn't be easy to discover your father was a monster. But Donovan's sympathy was limited. Karl Rivers had killed a man in cold blood and threatened to kill even more people. He deserved for his son to know all about his evil deeds. Too bad he wasn't there to see it.

Carson took a step closer to Donovan. "It says in here that you knew something about him. You'd seen something that made him run you out of town. That as long as you kept your mouth shut and didn't return, it would never be discovered. So what was it? What did you see?"

"I can't believe that's all it said." Actually, Donovan couldn't believe Karl Rivers had written any of it down. Maybe his arrogance had him believing he would get away with it. And in a way he had. Until now.

Faced with the opportunity to destroy Karl's image in his son's eyes, Donovan hesitated. Carson had been his friend. More than that, he'd cared for Raven and Elias when Donovan hadn't been around. That counted for something.

"No. He said that I'm the reason he went soft. He felt he owed you for the way you'd always protected his nerdy son. That he'd always hoped that if I hung around you long enough I'd become like you instead of the loser that I was." The pain was evident in Carson's voice and Donovan ached for him. Good old Karl Rivers, ruining lives from the grave.

"There was nothing wrong with the way you were. I was proud to call you my friend."

"I don't care about that," Carson yelled. His voice carried across the acres. He was on the verge of losing control. Still there was a determination in his stance. Donovan wasn't going to be able to divert him. And really, should he even try? Carson deserved the truth and Karl Rivers certainly didn't deserve protection. "I want to know what you knew that made him run you out of town."

"What?"

Donovan spun around. *Raven.* He'd been so focused on Carson that he hadn't heard her truck. She ignored Carson and stared at Donovan, never once breaking eye contact as she closed the distance between them. "What is Carson talking about? Who ran you out of town? Is that why you left me?"

"It's a long story. One I don't intend to tell while standing in the middle of the driveway."

"My father…" Carson interjected.

"What?" Raven looked shocked, but she was still standing. Maybe she was stronger than he'd given her credit for being.

"My father ran Donovan out of town." Carson's eyes moved from Raven to Donovan in under a second. "But what I don't know is what he held over you to make you go and never come back until he was dead. That is why you didn't come back until now, right? What was he so afraid of you telling?"

"Well?" Raven asked when Donovan only stood there. "I want to know, too. I put my life on hold for ten long years while I waited for you to come home. Don't you think I deserve the truth?"

"Fine. I'll explain everything." Donovan glanced at Carson. "You'd better be sure you want the truth. I can tell you now that you won't like it."

"I'm not a child. I no longer need your protection."

Donovan nodded. Instead of going inside, he led them to the backyard and across the grass to the corral. They leaned against the fence. Donovan focused on the horses.

"The day I left, I was going to town. This was before they built all those houses, so the road was deserted. I don't think I passed a car for miles. I drove past the main entrance to the Rivers Ranch and was near the isolated part of the ranch when I heard a gunshot. At first I thought it was a hunter. But then it occurred to me that it was private property and no one should be hunting out there. I knew Mr. Rivers would be pissed. Before I could think of what to do, a man stumbled into the road right in front of me. I slammed on the brakes, barely missing him. He was bleeding from his shoulder. He staggered to his feet and tried to get in the car."

"It's okay, Donovan," Raven said and gave his hand a gentle squeeze. He'd forgotten she was there. Forgotten Carson was there. Telling the story had set him right back on that road. He was nineteen years old and scared.

"Keep going." Carson's voice sounded flat and unemotional, but Donovan knew Carson was trying to mask the dread he had to be feeling, knowing what he was about to hear would be awful. Donovan admired Carson's determination to learn the truth no matter how painful.

Donovan blew out a breath. "The man put his hand on my passenger window. It was smeared with blood and left a red print behind. Then there was another gunshot. He jerked and slid to the ground. I was in a state of shock. I couldn't move."

Donovan heard the panic in his voice and breathed deeply. "The next thing I knew, someone was pulling me from my car. It was the sheriff."

"The sheriff?" Raven and Carson spoke at the same time.

"Yeah. Sheriff Brown. Karl Rivers was behind the other guy and he was holding a gun. He'd shot that other man in cold blood. The sheriff asked what Mr. Rivers wanted to do with me. Mr. Rivers said it was a shame

I had seen what I did. Now I was going to have to die, too. I begged and pleaded with him. I swore I wouldn't tell a soul what I'd seen. Ever. He was still pointing the gun at my chest. I thought he was going to shoot me, too. Then he lowered his gun. He said I had better leave town right then and stay gone. If I ever came back, he'd kill me, my parents and you, Raven."

"Me? Why?"

"Because he knew how much I loved you and that I would do anything to keep you safe."

Raven's eyes filled with tears. She blinked and the tears fell. Without thinking, he brushed the moisture from her soft skin. Then he remembered she was engaged and that her fiancé was standing beside them and dropped his hand. Not that Carson appeared to be aware of anything—he had a dazed look on his face.

"You know the rest of the story. I left and I didn't come back until I found out he was dead."

"I never heard of anyone being murdered," Raven said, then looked over at Carson. "Did you?"

He shook his head. "But…"

"But what?" Donovan demanded.

"My dad was acting strange around that time. I didn't pay much attention to it because that was around the time you disappeared. After a while he became his usual self again and I forgot about it."

They were silent for long minutes as Carson and Raven digested what they'd learned. After a while, Carson spoke to Donovan. "Are you sure about what you saw?"

"Perfectly. I know this is hard for you, but that's what happened. Your dad murdered someone in cold blood."

"I'm sorry for what my father did to you."

Donovan looked at the other man. He looked absolutely destroyed. "You don't need to apologize for him. You didn't threaten me and my loved ones and you certainly didn't kill that man. The guilt belongs to your father and him alone. Bury it with him."

"Did you recognize the—" Carson cleared his throat but his voice was still choked "—the man my father killed?"

"No. I never saw him before in my life. For all I know, he could have been someone who stumbled on your father and the sheriff doing something illegal and paid for it with his life."

Carson nodded absently. He didn't seem convinced. Perhaps it didn't line up with whatever else he'd read in the journal. "Maybe."

"Anyway. Now you know the truth."

Carson blew out a deep breath. "Yeah. I've got to go."

"Carson, wait." Raven reached for her fiancé but he stepped back before she could touch him.

"Not now, Raven."

"But…"

"No buts. I need some time."

"I can help."

"Help? How? I just learned my father was a murderer. You can't help with that. Just leave me alone." Carson turned and, without another word, stalked around the house to his car. A minute later the roar of a car engine filled the silence as he drove away.

Donovan leaned against the fence. Now that he'd told the entire story, he felt relieved. It was as if by saying the words the incident lost its power over him. He would tell the new sheriff what he'd seen and let the lawman handle matters from there.

"Why didn't you tell me?" Raven's voice trembled, whether with sorrow or fury, he couldn't tell.

"At first I was worried about you. You fainted the second you looked at me. I didn't think you could take another shock. I thought I'd give you time to adjust to having me around before dropping another surprise on you. Later you threatened to take me to court if I mentioned the past again. I didn't want to risk it."

"I really wouldn't have done it. I hope you know that."

"I didn't think you would, but Elias was too important for me to risk. Besides, what difference would it make? Nothing between us would have changed. I still would have been gone for ten years. I still would have missed my son's entire life. And you still would have been engaged to someone else. Now that you know the truth, have any of those things changed?"

Raven shook her head.

"I didn't think so." He watched his horses race through the grass before turning back to her. "Why did you come over? Last I knew, you weren't speaking to me. In fact, you hung up on me. Did Carson tell you he was on his way here and ask you to meet him?"

"No." She handed him an envelope. "I brought pictures of Elias."

"Really? I thought you said if I'd wanted to see Elias grow up I should have hung around."

"I'm sorry. I didn't know the truth."

He nudged her. The fact that she'd changed her mind before she'd found out what really happened made him happier than it should have. "I'm kidding, Raven. Thanks."

"Are you going to open them now or do you want to look at them alone?"

He opened the envelope and pulled out a small stack of pictures. On top was a photo of a toothless baby with a wide grin. His hands were open and he was reaching out. Raven leaned over and rested her head on Donovan's shoulder. Her sweet scent reached his nostrils and he inhaled deeply. It had been years since she'd been this close to him. Years since she'd put her head on his shoulder. He was tempted to wrap his arm around her waist and pull her closer, but he didn't. Their time had ended long ago. She was engaged to another man. She'd moved on and he needed to do the same. It was time to get on with his life.

Chapter Nine

"What is he doing here?" Donovan asked, holding a picture out so Raven could see it. Elias had his arms out to the side and one foot off the ground.

The picture brought back fond memories and she smiled. "He's trying to convince me to let him walk on the fence. He's showing me how good his balance is."

"Oh. How old is he in this picture? Six?"

Raven nodded.

"I remember walking across this very fence at that age."

"And falling off a lot, as I recall." She looked at him pointedly. "You spent more time on the ground than on the rail."

"Yep. Balance wasn't my strong suit. If I remember correctly you managed to do it on your first try."

"Not really," she confessed with a grin. "I have four older brothers, remember? I had to keep up with them.

I'd been walking the fence at home for years before we tried here."

"And you never said a word. My poor damaged male ego took quite a hit that day. A girl was able to do something I couldn't."

"And yet you survived."

He laughed. "Barely. Luckily none of the other boys could do it, either. So how did Elias do? Did he inherit your grace or my lack thereof?"

"I didn't let him try."

"Why not? Don't tell me you turned into one of those overprotective mothers who don't let their kids do anything fun?"

"Not a chance. I told him no because he wanted to do it blindfolded."

"Blindfolded?"

"Yep. He'd read a book about circus performers and wanted to see how it felt to walk the tightrope blindfolded. He was skipping the baby stuff and going for the gusto. He was positive he could do it. If you look closer, you'll see his bicycle. After he walked across blindfolded, he was planning to ride across the same way."

Donovan threw back his head and roared with laughter. The sound brought back happy memories the two of them had shared. They'd been lovers, but they'd been so much more than that. They'd been best friends. He'd understood her better than anyone else ever had.

Raven had always been a tomboy. Growing up, she'd preferred to ride her horse, fish and hunt. She'd never played dress-up or with dolls and couldn't name a single Disney princess. As a result, she'd had more in common with the boys her age than with the girls.

Even as a teenager, when other girls had been doing

things to attract boys like wearing fancy clothes and perfume, she'd stuck with her jeans and T-shirts. She hadn't polished her nails and hadn't bothered with makeup. She hadn't spent money getting her hair done because she'd only pull it back into a ponytail and out of her way. That had been fine with Donovan. He'd been proud of who she was and hadn't ever tried to change her. That had only made her love him more.

She glanced over at him. He was staring at another picture, a wistful expression on his face. He touched Elias's image. "I wish I could have been there."

"I know." She squeezed his arm. She felt bad about having been so rough on him when he'd first come back. She should have known he'd had a good reason for leaving her. "You're here now."

"I know I should be content with being a part of his life now, but I can't. I want more."

A chill raced down her spine. She'd threatened him with a lawyer. Would he do the same? "Are you going to try to take him from me?"

"What?" He sounded positively appalled at the idea and her heart slowed back to normal. "Of course not. I just want to be able to tell him who I am."

"I know. You can. But we need to take it slow."

"Yeah." He turned, leaned his back against the fence and stared across the green field. "When can I see him again?"

"He's spending the day with Kenny. Kenny's dad is taking them back to the carnival, but he'll have him home by eight." She took a deep breath and hesitated before continuing. Once she said the words there would be no taking them back. "If you want to come over around then, you can."

Donovan's face lit up then fell. "Won't it look suspicious if I just happen to turn up at the same time as he does? What am I supposed to do, ask to borrow a cup of sugar?"

The bitterness and frustration in his voice saddened her. She'd be heartbroken if she'd been the one to miss out on Elias's life. "Okay. Well, how about you come over for dinner tomorrow? And you won't need a reason. You're an old friend and we're catching up. He has dinner with his friends, so it won't appear odd to him."

"And Carson? How is he going to feel? He was pretty upset. This isn't going to make him feel better. If anything, it might look like we're piling on."

She blew out a breath. It might be complicated, but her dad was right. One thing had nothing to do with the other. She couldn't in good conscience keep Donovan from spending time with his son, especially now that she knew why he'd stayed away. Besides, with everything Carson had to be feeling, Donovan was probably the least of his concerns. "I'll talk to him. He knows you're Elias's father."

"In that case, yes."

"Good. We eat at five thirty, so come around then. Okay?"

"Yes."

"I'd better get going." She walked to her truck. Her heart leaped as she thought about Donovan joining her and Elias for dinner. They were going to have their very first family dinner. She tried to tell herself it was not a big deal, but she wasn't convinced.

But she was convinced of one thing. She needed to end her engagement to Carson. Marrying him wouldn't be fair to either of them. Simply being around Donovan made her remember what it felt like to be in love. How good it felt to love and be loved. She didn't feel that way about Carson and she'd be short-changing both of them if she went through with the wedding.

Not that she was still in love with Donovan. Memories of being in love and actually being in love were two different things. Just because they'd loved each other ten years ago didn't mean they could pick up where they'd left off and magically fall in love again. Even she knew that love didn't work that way. It needed to be nurtured. She knew the feeling that she'd held on to so tightly all those years wasn't love. It was fear of feeling a hurt so strong it might overwhelm her. A hurt she didn't think she would ever get over. But that was a problem for another time. She had to end this relationship.

The question was when would she do it? Carson was hurting so badly now, it would be cruel to add to it. Besides, he would need someone to lean on. Who else could he count on if not his fiancée? Especially since she knew the whole sordid story.

When she got home, she sat on her front porch. Maybe working a crossword puzzle or two would help her think. But instead of opening the chest to get out her puzzle book, she stared off into the distance.

An hour or so later, Carson drove up. Apparently he'd changed his mind about wanting to be alone.

"How are you?" She could have slapped her forehead. That was a stupid question. He looked just as devastated as he'd been the last time she'd seen him. Not that she expected anything different. Who wouldn't be destroyed after discovering their father was a murderer. She still was struggling to wrap her mind around what Donovan had said and knew she would be for some time. It would be even harder for Carson to accept. Philanthropist, political donor and *father* Karl Rivers had been a murderer. He'd actually threatened her life and then had the audacity to refer to her as his future daughter. The very idea that she'd actually shared meals with that monster turned her stomach.

"I've been better." His eyes were red and she imagined he'd spent time crying.

She let her nod suffice as her response. The last thing she wanted to do was to spout banalities. She knew tomorrow wouldn't be better. His life would never be the same. "Did you tell your mother?"

"No. And I'd appreciate if you didn't say anything, either. She'll need to know eventually, but I'd rather she heard it from me."

"Of course. I'm not going to tell a soul. I don't think Donovan will, either, if that's what you're worried about."

He gave her an odd look. "*I'm* going to say something. Somewhere out there a man's family is wondering what happened to him. Another woman could be out there hoping he'll come home to her. She could feel the same way you did all these years. Unfortunately for her, there won't be a happy ending. Even so, she deserves to know the truth. She deserves to know that he was murdered and that it was covered up for years."

"I hadn't thought of it that way. The police need to be told. I was only thinking of you and your mother."

"We'll be okay. Knowing the truth is always better than living a lie, don't you think?"

She rubbed her hands on her denim-clad thighs. "Yes. Are we still talking about your father?"

"No. Not exclusively."

"Then what?"

"You aren't in love with me, Raven. I thought it would be enough that I was in love with you. And maybe it would have been if Donovan hadn't come home. Just like everyone else, I thought he was dead. And if you still loved him…well that was all right. He was a ghost. Sooner or later you'd let him go and your feelings would fade away. I had the rest of our lives to convince you. You'd see how well I'd treat you, what a good stepfather I was to Elias, and you'd eventually fall in love with me." He shook his head and looked at her with sad eyes. "But that's not going to happen."

"No," she whispered. "It's not. But it's not because of Donovan. We aren't still in love."

"Maybe not yet."

"I'm not even thinking about that. So much time has passed. We're not the same people we were ten years ago. And Donovan is focused on getting to know Elias."

"Something he wouldn't have to worry about if not for my father."

She stared him in the eye. "That's right. Your father is to blame. Not you. Don't carry his guilt on your shoulders. That's a burden you don't deserve to bear."

He took her left hand and brushed her ring finger. "You never did wear your ring."

"I work on a ranch. I didn't want to risk losing it."

"Maybe. Or maybe it was a sign that we weren't meant to be married. The reason doesn't matter now."

Maybe he was right. Perhaps part of her had known they weren't meant to be together. If only she had listened, she wouldn't be hurting him right now. "I'll get it. It's in my jewelry box."

"Okay."

She raced upstairs and came back with the ring. The princess-cut diamond really was beautiful. It just hadn't ever felt right on her finger.

He slipped the ring into the front pocket of his jeans as if it was a cheap, plastic bauble he'd won at the carnival. "I'm going to be leaving in a couple of days. I'm taking my mother to stay with her sister in Atlanta. Then I'm going to try to identify the man Donovan saw murdered and find his family."

She kissed his cheek. "That's an honorable thing to do. You're a good man, Carson Rivers."

"Thanks."

The pain in his voice made her heart ache. He'd been there for her when she'd needed him yet she was powerless to help him now. She hoped he'd find someone who could help him deal with his feelings. A good man, he deserved that much.

Donovan switched the bouquet of wildflowers from one hand to the other. On his walk through Sweet Briar the other day, he'd come upon a florist, Pretty Blooming Things, and had taken a quick look inside just in case he ever wanted to buy anyone flowers.

Looking at the pink and purple flowers, two of Raven's favorite colors, he wondered if he'd made a mistake. This wasn't a date. Raven had invited him to dinner so that he could spend time with his son. For all he knew, Carson would be there, as well. And even if he wasn't, Carson and Raven were still engaged. Donovan didn't want her to think he didn't respect her relationship or that he was trying to win her back. Nothing could be further from the truth.

He could hear footsteps inside the house growing

near and knew he didn't have time to put the bouquet in the car. Looking around, he spotted the chest near the wicker furniture. Before he could change his mind, he raced over, opened the chest and tossed the flowers inside. He made it to the door just as it swung open.

Raven smiled at him and his heart danced a silly jig. For a moment he was seventeen again and coming courting as his father called it when he'd teased Donovan. It probably hadn't been called courting even when his father was a teenager.

"Were you running?"

"Running? Why would I be running?"

She shrugged.

"I hope I'm not too early."

"Not at all. Elias is always ready to eat. My folks went to Heaven on Earth with some friends, so it'll just be the three of us."

"What's Heaven on Earth?"

"Only the best restaurant in the entire state. And it's right here in Sweet Briar. Brandon Danielson, a chef from Chicago, moved here a few years ago and opened a restaurant."

"Really?" He'd missed so much while he'd been gone. The little town he remembered had grown a lot. Many of the businesses he remembered, like the diner, were still there, so Sweet Briar was still recognizable. But while he'd recognized a lot of the older people he'd encountered, there were a lot of strangers. He had a lot of catching up to do.

"Yes." Raven walked through the house to the kitchen, so he followed her. His eyes were drawn to the sweet curve of her hips. As usual, she was wearing jeans that hugged her bottom and showcased her shapely legs.

The table was set for three. "I figured we'd just eat in here, if that's okay with you?"

"Fine by me." The location didn't matter. He'd be happy sitting in the mud if he still got to eat dinner with Raven and his son.

"And you'll never guess who he's married to," Raven said as she pulled a pan of macaroni and cheese from the oven and set it on top of the stove.

"Who are you talking about?"

"Brandon Danielson. The chef at Heaven on Earth?"

"Oh. Right. Who is he married to?"

"Arden *Wexford*."

"Of the hotel Wexfords?" The Wexfords were one of the wealthiest families in America.

"Yep. You won't believe how they met. Her car broke down and he rescued her. She used a fake last name and worked as a waitress in his restaurant. She even rented his garage apartment. Boy, he was furious when he found out who she really was. He even fired her. There was quite a scandal. You missed everything." She looked up, her eyes wide with concern. "I'm so sorry. I didn't mean that the way it sounded."

"I know. The truth is, I did miss it. I missed a lot of things."

"I could just kick that Karl Rivers for what he did to you."

"You have to let it go. It's in the past. Being angry won't change anything."

Raven grabbed a salad from the refrigerator and set it on the center of the table. Then she looked right at him. "Have you let it go?"

"Not entirely, but I'm getting there. For the longest time I was filled with hate and anger and so many other negative emotions that I can't name. Once I stopped being scared, it occurred to me that I spent every hour of every day being angry. I couldn't come home without risking your lives, something that I wasn't willing to do. But that didn't mean I couldn't have a life where I was. If I stayed angry and didn't even try to belong anywhere, I was letting him take even more from me than he already had."

"So did you?"

"It took some doing, but yes. I let go of the anger. Don't get me wrong, I didn't forgive Rivers or stop hating him with every fiber of my being. I just stopped being angry."

"That's not what I meant?"

"Then what do you mean?"

"Did you find a place to belong? Settle down? Have a family?"

"I never married, if that's what you're asking. And I don't have any other children, either."

"But did you find a place to belong? Please say you did. I hate the idea of you wandering from place to place, spending all your time alone."

"I did find a place but not at first. For a long time I was afraid to stay in one place. I thought Karl Rivers had someone following me. I was worried that he'd changed his mind and decided to kill me, so I pretty much did what Arden Wexford did. I used a fake name and got a few jobs off the books. When I'd get nervous, I'd move on. I didn't get close to anyone, so nobody cared when I left."

"That's terrible. And so sad."

"Yeah. Eventually I ended up in Texas. I worked on a couple of different ranches before I came upon Della and Gabe Turner's place. They own about two hundred thousand acres and run ten thousand head of cattle. I figured that since the place was so big, I'd be able to blend into the background. Boy, was I mistaken." He smiled. "They may have a big operation, but they get to know their employees. They treat everyone like family."

"Really?" Raven sounded skeptical and he couldn't blame her. In other places he would have been a cog in a wheel.

"Yes. Della and Gabe actually meet all the new hires face-to-face. There weren't many of us because it's a wonderful place to work and not many people quit. The other new employees had families and ties to the area. I was the only one with nobody."

"Oh, Donovan."

"It's okay. This really was a happy time in my life. When Della and Gabe realized I didn't have a family, they sort of adopted me. Della invited me to Sunday dinner so many times. I kept saying no. Then Christmas came and I was all alone. I'd endured three Christmases alone already. One year I'd found a church that served dinner to the homeless and gave out little gifts. The other two years I managed to ignore Christmas altogether. But this year was different. I felt so lonely.

"I wasn't surprised when Della invited me to dinner. I said no at first but then I changed my mind. When I walked into the kitchen, everyone said hi and treated me like I belonged. Della and Gabe have a big family. Several of the older sons were married and had little kids of their own. But they had two college-age sons who were home for winter break. They're good guys and we ended up shooting pool and playing video games. We became really good friends." Friends he'd left behind and had yet to contact. He'd call them soon.

"And the Turners had one daughter. She was the youngest child and a handful."

"Oh yeah?"

"Amelia was such a girlie-girl. You would never guess she lived on a ranch. Anyway, she was fifteen. When her brothers left, they made me promise to keep an eye on her."

"I'm sure she loved that," Raven said dryly.

"About as much as you would have. But they'd taken me in as family and I promised I would. Once I made it clear I had no intention of interfering in her life, we got along great. Especially on those occasions when she needed a ride to town."

"So it wasn't all bad? You were actually happy sometime?"

"Yes."

Raven suddenly got busy rearranging the silverware on the napkins. "Did you ever fall in love?"

"No. I never even came close. What did I have to offer anyone? A fake name? A lifetime of hiding?" He put his hand on hers, stilling her nervous activity. "Truth be told, I didn't want to fall in love again. I didn't want to take the risk."

"That Karl Rivers would threaten your new girl-friend the way he threatened your parents and me?"

"No. I didn't want to risk loving someone and losing her again. I knew my heart couldn't take it."

Chapter Ten

Raven didn't know how to respond to that statement. Fortunately for her, Elias walked into the kitchen just then and she didn't have to.

"Is it time to eat yet? I'm starving."

"Did you wash your hands?"

"Yep."

"Then sit down."

"Hey, Donovan. I didn't know you were here."

"Your Mom invited me for dinner. I hope that's okay."

Elias smiled as he pulled out his chair and sat. "Sure."

Donovan held Raven's chair. She glanced up at him and smiled. "Thanks."

After saying the blessing, Raven scooped up a spoonful of peas and reached for Elias's plate. He scooted it away from her grasp. "Donovan is our guest. You should serve him first, you know, in case we run out of peas."

As Donovan's laughter mingled with hers, Raven became uncomfortably aware of just how well he fit in with her and Elias. Though he had just met their son, and he'd been separated from her for a decade, there wasn't any awkwardness. Telling herself it was good that they got on so well, she picked up Elias's plate and loaded it with a good helping of peas. They weren't his favorite vegetable, but he usually buried them in his other food and ate them without too much fuss. Salad, on the other hand, was another story, which was why she wasn't even going to try.

"Thank you," Elias said after she'd added macaroni and cheese, roast and homemade rolls to his plate.

"Help yourself," she said to Donovan before filling her own plate.

She was quiet as she ate, half listening as Donovan and Elias talked about the latest superhero movie. It was coming out in nine days and Elias had been begging her to take him on opening night. That way he would be the first of all of his friends to see it, which was important to him. Since Sweet Briar didn't have a movie theater, and it wasn't showing at the theater in nearby Willow Creek, and they'd have to drive two hours to Charlotte, the closest place it was showing, he could see it later in the month and still stand a good chance of being the first of his friends to see it.

"You should come with me and Mom when we go," Elias said, snatching her attention back to the conversation.

"When are you going?"

"Opening night."

Raven sputtered. "I never said we were going."

"You didn't say we weren't. Besides, I already invited Donovan. It would be bad manners to take it back now."

Donovan made a choking noise that sounded suspiciously like laughter. He might think the situation was funny now, but she couldn't wait until he had to deal with a nine-year-old who was too smart for his own good. She'd be the one laughing. A day ago that thought might have shocked her. Sure she knew co-parenting Elias was the only fair thing to do. But being able to work together with laughter and friendship was even better than she could have hoped.

"I'll think about it. Donovan might have other plans."

"Do you?" Elias asked. He seemed to be holding his breath, waiting for Donovan's answer.

Strangely enough, she was holding her breath, too.

"No plans at all."

"Then it's settled. We're going to the movies." Elias chased the last pea around his plate with his fork then squished it with the tines. He didn't lift it to his mouth. "I'm done. Do you think Grandma and Granddad will bring me back some dessert?"

"I doubt it. You'll have to settle for cookies and milk."

"Okay." He dumped a handful of cookies into a paper towel and refilled his cup. "See you later, Donovan."

"I expect to see that cup in the sink before the night is over," Raven said as Elias sprinted from the kitchen.

"I know. You will."

"He's a terrific kid," Donovan said when they were alone. "You've done a great job with him."

"It wasn't me alone. My parents did most of it when

he was a baby. I didn't have a clue how to care for him. I was barely able to care for myself."

"Because you were stressed out about me?"

"Yes. It wasn't until I realized Elias was turning to them to get his needs met instead of me that I knew I had to do better. It was a struggle to hold myself together enough to be the mother he deserved, but I did it."

Donovan stared into his lemonade before taking a swallow. "I hope I didn't overstep about the movie. I'm just trying to find a way to fit in his life."

"Not at all. You're his father. You belong in his life. The fact that you're just as invested in superheroes as him is a bonus. My father wouldn't know the Green Lantern from the Green Hornet. In fact, I doubt he's heard of either of them."

"And Carson?"

His question was tentatively asked, as if he was worried about stepping on her toes again. They might have had a good dinner, but neither of them was sure of their footing. It would take time for them to find their way. "He wasn't really a fan. That won't be an issue in the future. He ended our engagement."

"Because of what I told you?" He sounded shocked and guilty.

"No. Not at all."

"Then why, if you don't mind my asking? Karl Rivers was a murderer, but from what I could tell, Carson is nothing like him."

"He's not." Raven was too confused about everything to discuss the matter any further. She and Carson had done the right thing by ending their engagement, but she still felt bad for having hurt him. "I'd prefer not to talk about this, if you don't mind."

"No problem. I understand. I know we're only beginning to rebuild our friendship but I'm here if you want to talk."

"Thanks."

Donovan drained his glass, stood and put his dishes into the sink. "And on that note, I'd better get going. We both have to get up early tomorrow."

She followed him to the door and stepped onto the porch. It was a nice night, so she might just sit outside for a while. He seemed unsure of himself, lingering on the porch for a moment before descending the stairs. He looked back at her before getting into his pickup and driving away.

She crossed the porch and sat on the cushioned love seat. She'd been aghast when her mother had replaced the old, familiar porch swing with this new furniture. After spending a couple of quiet evenings out here, she'd seen the wisdom of her mother's way. The furniture was very comfortable and relaxing and Raven found herself spending more time out here than she had before. Best of all, the chest that doubled as a table provided precious storage, holding one of her mother's handmade quilts for cooler nights.

Tonight, though, she only wanted to enjoy the tranquil evening. The sun had set and the stars were becoming visible in the indigo sky. Lightning bugs flittered in the growing darkness. This was her favorite time of the day. She loved the tranquility. Elias was ensconced in his room, happily reading one of his many books, and she had some time alone. Usually that would be enough for her to relax, but tonight there was a nagging sense of disquiet.

She'd expected to feel a bit sad about her broken engagement and she did. Carson had been a good, supportive friend and he was hurting. Deep down she knew they'd done the right thing. He deserved a wife who would love him with her whole heart. A wife who wanted his love and devotion. Raven wasn't that woman and never would be. Ending the relationship would give him the opportunity to find the right one.

Now that things had been set right between them, she should be at peace, but she wasn't. It didn't take long to recognize the source of her unrest. She'd just spent the last few hours with him. Donovan Cordero. She'd been restless since he'd come back into her life.

She'd often dreamed of the day he would return, but nothing was the way she'd imagined it would be. In those dreams, they'd taken one look at each other and fallen into each other's arms. Nothing close to that had happened. Okay, she'd gotten a little bit woozy and he'd carried her to the couch, but that didn't count.

Her dreams had never included anger and resentment. She hadn't even known she'd harbored those feelings until they'd consumed her. She'd been glad to have him back, but she'd resented him for staying away for so long. Now that she knew it wasn't by choice, most of the resentment was gone, but a stubborn remnant held on. Hopefully she could shake it soon.

In her fantasies, she'd never accounted for the fact that they would be different people. Ten years had changed them. Of course, maturity caused some of the differences. But they'd lived different lives and seen different things. They hadn't shared a single experience in ten years. They were more different than they would have been had they been together the past decade.

Yet different or not, there was something about him

that appealed to her. A certain elemental something that called to her on a basic level. But was it real? Was the part of her that had refused to let go of him manufacturing the attraction? Was she trying to convince herself that they belonged together because she'd spent a decade waiting for him to come back to her? She didn't know. But she was old enough and wise enough to know that pretending they were still in love would be a mistake.

The truth was, despite their agreement to put the past behind them, it was still questionable whether they would get along. Right now they were being polite, feeling each other out. Would they even like each other after they set down their company manners? If the answer was no, co-parenting could become difficult.

That was enough thinking. She'd worry about the future when it arrived. The present was complicated enough. She headed into the house and the distraction of the television. Hopefully she would find something compelling enough to remove every thought of Donovan Cordero.

"What are we going to do today?" Elias asked.

Raven sighed. This was so unlike her son. Generally he found ways to entertain himself. He was either helping her father or reading. Kenny had gone to visit his grandparents on the last day of school and would be there until the end of the week. Elias had other friends, but most of them lived in town, an hour away from the ranch. The youth center had a lot of activities for kids, but again it was in town. Raven didn't like the idea of leaving him at the youth center all day, but it didn't make sense to spend two hours in the car if he was only going to spend a few hours there.

"What do you want to do?" He was old enough to come up with ideas of how to occupy himself.

"I was thinking we could go for a horseback ride. We haven't done that in a long time."

His definition of a long time differed from hers. They'd gone riding just last week. But since she did enjoy riding with him, she didn't quibble. She could fit in a ride and still get her work done. "That sounds like a plan. Get changed and meet me in the stables in fifteen minutes."

Elias was dashing from the room before she'd finished her sentence. He was just as crazy about riding his horse as he was about superheroes. He'd grown bored of riding on the acres near the house, but he was too young for her to consider letting him ride to the far reaches of the ranch by himself.

She rummaged through the refrigerator and pulled out leftover fried chicken and cold cuts. In under ten minutes she put together a large lunch then met Elias in the stables. He'd saddled Evening Dream as well as his horse, Dark Knight, and was holding them by the reins.

As they mounted their horses she asked, "Which way do you want to ride today?"

He didn't hesitate but pointed toward the Cordero ranch. "That way."

She hadn't ridden that way since the night she'd forced her heart to say goodbye to Donovan. Of course, that goodbye had turned out to have been a bit premature. She wondered if her letting go of Donovan and his unexpected return were somehow linked. She shook her head. That was a crazy idea.

"Why not?"

"What? Oh, I wasn't saying no to you. That's a good idea. Let's go."

As they went, Raven took time to actually look at the ranch. It really was beautiful. She might be biased, but their ranch was the most scenic in all of North Carolina. The grass was a deep shade of green and the trees were mature, filled with thousands of leaves. There was nothing but untouched beauty as far as the eye could see.

After about twenty minutes they came upon several deer drinking from a stream. A ranch kid used to being exposed to nature, Elias stopped talking so as not to startle them. The deer continued drinking for another minute or so. When they'd had their fill, they ran away, disappearing into the trees.

"Do you think Donovan is home?" Elias asked out of the blue.

"I guess. He's working on his family's ranch again."

"We should stop by. He might want to ride with us. And you brought a lot of food. We could share our lunch with him."

"Their ranch is really big. We might not be able to find him."

"Can we try?"

"I don't see why not. But remember, even if we do find him, he might not be able to hang out with us. He has work to do."

After riding for a while without seeing him, Raven was going to suggest they turn around. Then she saw him in the distance. He was sitting on a stallion, talking to two ranch hands who were repairing a fence.

Raven took the opportunity to get a good look at him. Majestic wasn't a word she normally used, but it suited him. Dressed in a light blue button-down shirt that looked tailored for his muscular torso and well-worn jeans, he could have been a male model in an ad for the outdoor lifestyle. His hat partially obscured his handsome face, but she could see it in her mind's eye.

When he finished talking, he turned and spotted them. He smiled as he expertly guided his horse in their direction, quickly closing the distance between them. He and his horse moved as one. It had been so long since she'd seen Donovan on a horse that she'd forgotten what an expert rider he was.

"To what do I owe the pleasure?" he asked when they were close enough to communicate without yelling.

"We've come to invite you to lunch," Raven said. "That is, if you have the time and haven't eaten yet."

"No, I haven't eaten. And yes, I always have time for you."

Raven's heart stuttered although she believed he probably meant her *and* Elias, not just her. "Great."

"Did you have a particular destination in mind or were you just looking for a good place to sit down?"

"We were looking for you," Elias said.

"Is that right?" Donovan shot Raven a sly grin before turning to their son. "Looks like you found me. I haven't had time to just ride for the fun of it since I got back. I visited one special place my first night back, but that's about it. Every other ride has been work."

Raven's stomach tumbled as the thought of the night she'd gone to their place. She did a quick calculation in her mind and determined that he'd been at their spot on the same night. What would she have done if she'd seen Donovan that night? What would he have done? Did it mean anything that both of them had felt drawn to the spot? The idea was too complicated to think about now.

"Do you have any other special places?" Elias asked.

"Too many to choose from. Maybe we can make a special place just for us three."

"Yeah," Elias said.

They went silent and she realized they were looking at her and waiting for a response, so she nodded.

They began riding away from the Cordero family home in a direction that led farther away from the more traveled part of the ranch to a hilly area. The terrain became more rugged and steep and they slowed down so that the horses could pick their way more carefully up the incline. Donovan was leading the way with Elias right behind him and Raven bringing up the rear where she could watch him. Not that she needed to worry. Elias was a good rider. More than that, Donovan was keeping an eye on him, as well.

After a few minutes they'd reached the top of the hill. From this vantage point they were able to see the vast expanse that was the Cordero ranch. Cattle grazed in the distance, looking like dark specks against the green grass.

"Wow," Raven said, sliding from her horse. "This is what I call a view. I'd forgotten how beautiful everything looks from a distance."

"Me, too. While I was away I tried to picture the ranch. Sometimes I could, but I could never capture the feeling that came from being here. As time went by, I lost the ability to remember what it looked like. There was only one place that I could picture."

"Here?"

He shook his head. "You know better than that. Our spot. Sometimes I could see it so vividly I felt like I could reach out and touch our tree. Touch you."

Donovan reached out and caressed her arm. Though

her blouse had long sleeves, she felt the heat from his fingers. His eyes met hers and held. The heat in them startled her and she took a step back. He immediately dropped his hand and turned away. A second had passed before she realized he'd interpreted her moving away as rejection. It wasn't. Before she could correct him, he'd walked away and struck up a conversation with Elias.

Perhaps it was for the best. She didn't know what she was doing and she certainly didn't want to further complicate the situation. Not only that, they hadn't told Elias that Donovan was his father. They needed to do that soon. At first she hadn't trusted Donovan, but that fear had been put to rest. She'd also been concerned that Donovan and Elias might not get along, but that clearly wasn't the case. After they'd gotten over their initial wariness, they'd clicked. She didn't foresee any problems with telling Elias the truth. She'd make sure Donovan agreed before she said anything.

Donovan and Elias found a spot they determined was just right for lunch and took it upon themselves to unpack the food. Donovan spread the quilt she'd packed on the ground and gestured for her to take a seat. As she approached, he smiled and whatever distance she'd unintentionally put between them vanished. She decided to enjoy the moment and not worry about what would happen between them. If there was one thing the past had taught her it was that she wasn't in control. No matter how carefully she planned, life took unexpected twists and turns. It was better to buckle up and go along for the ride.

Donovan watched Raven from the corner of his eye. She was nothing if not a bundle of contradictions. One minute she was keeping him at a distance and the next she was inviting him to dinner or showing up for a surprise lunch. For a moment today, it had been like old times. When they'd been younger, she'd often brought him lunch while he was repairing fence along their shared property line. Of course in those days, she'd have been just as likely to be working alongside him. She'd always joked that he'd starve if not for her. He'd been trying to win her heart, so he'd never told her that he'd had lunch in his saddlebag.

Elias grabbed his plate, then wandered away to watch the cattle.

"Don't go too far," Raven called. The wind blew her hair into her face and she brushed it behind her ear impatiently. Raven was so beautiful, but didn't seem to notice. Or maybe she did know—she'd be blind not to see how gorgeous she was—but didn't care. Appearances had never been the most important thing to her, not hers or anyone else's. It was what was inside that mattered to her. What the heart held that was reflected in a person's actions. That's what Raven cared about.

Those things mattered to Donovan, too. A pretty face could mask an ugly heart. But he wouldn't say that Raven's outward beauty didn't appeal to him. Her unblemished dark brown face, with high cheekbones, bright, clear brown eyes and full lips entranced him. And when she flashed a smile, he couldn't help but notice her straight, white teeth.

Her slim, curvy body with her firm bottom and slender legs was perfect. He'd seen plenty of women in his lifetime, but none had come close to comparing to Raven. True, he hadn't been in a position to start a relationship, but even if he had been, he'd known that none of the women could ever measure up to Raven. Over time he'd convinced himself that he'd inflated her appeal. Like the fisherman recounting the story of the fish that had grown larger with each retelling, he'd believed that Raven had become more beautiful each time he thought of her. He'd been wrong. If anything, he'd underplayed her beauty.

Although he wasn't ready to commit to anything— there was still too much of the past lingering in the air and too much uncertainty about the future—he was beginning to wonder if his teenage self hadn't been wiser than he'd known. Maybe Raven was not only more wonderful than he'd remembered, maybe she was the person who was right for him. Perhaps she was the person he could fall in love with again.

Then he recalled the way she'd recoiled at his touch. He might be considering rekindling their relationship, but she certainly wasn't. Touching her had been like grabbing a live wire. It had been electric. Sparks had shot through his body all the way to his toes. He was amazed that his hair wasn't standing on end. What had been such a thrilling thing hadn't affected Raven at all. At least, not positively if the way she'd moved away from him had been anything to go by.

But then, she'd been engaged only a few days ago. Carson had been the one to end the relationship, not her. Perhaps she was still in love with him and hoping they'd get back together again. It was possible that Raven believed that once he'd dealt with his shock and horror they'd reunite.

Donovan gritted his teeth. Despite what he'd told Raven, he hadn't completely gotten over his anger at Karl Rivers. Just thinking about the man enraged him.

"What's wrong," Raven asked.

Donovan looked at her. "Nothing."

"Really? You're mangling that sandwich. If you squeeze it any tighter, the turkey is going to come flying from between the buns."

"Sorry." He loosened his grip on the destroyed sandwich and took a bite. "It still tastes good."

"I guess you don't know your own strength." Her eyes flicked over his body before meeting his. There was mischief in her expression. "You've filled out. Perhaps you're still getting used to your new muscles."

He laughed and flexed his biceps. "I'll have you know, I was born with this physique. Perhaps your memory is faulty."

"Faulty, my foot. I was stronger than you were."

"Please." He reached out and placed the back of his hand against her forehead. "You're not warm, so you don't have a fever. You should have worn a hat. You've had too much sun."

"Ha. Very funny. You might not remember all of the times I beat you at wrestling but I do. I could pin you in under a minute."

"We were eight years old." And she'd had the benefit of older brothers who'd showed her no mercy when they were roughhousing. They'd never treated her like a delicate little girl, so she hadn't been one. She'd been one heck of an athlete, better at just about everything than all of the boys their age.

"We were nine. Not that it matters. I still hold the record for beating you." She laughed and raised her hands over her head in victory and began to sing. "I am the champion of the world."

He tossed a crust of bread at her and of course she

caught it. Mercifully she stopped trying to sing. "I want a rematch."

"Not a chance." She tried to scoot away, but he was too fast for her. He didn't want to risk hurting her by grabbing her arm in case she tried to twist away so he wrapped his arms around her tiny waist and brought her closer to him. Her sweet scent encircled him and, just like that, he was nineteen years old again. It was as if the intervening ten years had only been ten minutes. The familiar longing for her was almost too much to control. He lowered her to the ground and leaned over her, gently pinning her shoulders to the blanket. "I win."

Their eyes met and held. Neither of them moved. Slowly he lowered his head, bringing his lips within an inch of hers.

"Are you trying to kiss my mom?"

Chapter Eleven

Donovan momentarily froze then jerked into an up-right position. He'd forgotten all about Elias; he must have come back while Donovan and Raven were distracted. "Uh. No. We were just playing."

"It doesn't look like playing to me."

"Actually we were wrestling," Raven said. She sat up smoothly and reached for her bottle of water. Donovan noticed that her hand trembled slightly. Apparently she wasn't as unaffected as she pretended. "I used to beat Donovan at wrestling all the time and he was trying to beat me now. Of course he had to cheat in order to pin me."

"My mom can beat you wrestling?" Elias looked scandalized.

"Of course not. This happened a long time ago when we were kids. We were only eight."

"Nine," Raven corrected.

Elias hooted. "You got beat by a girl."

"Your mom isn't just any girl. She's special." Donovan glanced over at Raven again. Her smile widened at the compliment and she dipped her head slightly in acknowledgment. "She's got superpowers. She can make even the strongest man weak as a baby."

Elias seemed unconvinced by the argument. He tugged on his ear. "Or maybe you were just weak when you were nine. Maybe your muscles hadn't come in yet. I heard some boys don't get strong until they're ten."

"Not you, though."

"Nah. I've been strong since I was seven."

Donovan managed to keep a straight face. "You probably inherited your mother's superpowers. That's possible, you know."

Elias shrugged before looking at Donovan seriously. "Don't be ashamed because my mom was stronger than you when you were a kid. That was a long time ago. Mom always says you can't change the past, so just put it behind you and try to do better now." He frowned as if uncertain his words applied in this situation. "But she usually says that after I do something wrong and say I'm sorry. Anyway, the important thing is that you're strong now."

Donovan nodded at the pep talk. Elias was talking about one thing, but Donovan knew he'd have to apply that attitude to everything in his life. If not, he'd walk around angry, thinking about everything he'd missed. "I agree. And as you can see, I'm stronger than your mom now."

Elias grabbed a cookie and walked away. He turned, a wide grin on his face as he called back, "Unless she uses her superpowers on you."

Donovan watched until he was sure that Elias was too far away to hear him speak, even with super hearing. "Should I apologize?"

"For what? Cheating?"

Donovan grinned at her attempt to keep it light. He was tempted to do so, as well, but decided against it. Since time travel was out of the question, his superpower was going to be honesty. "No. For overstepping. If Elias hadn't interrupted, I would have kissed you. I just want to know if, given your situation, that would have been wrong."

"What situation?"

"Carson broke your engagement. That had to have hurt. I don't want to be the jerk who swoops in trying to take advantage of your broken heart. Not that I'm trying to do that."

"I know. To be honest, my heart isn't broken. Not in the way you think. I'm sad because of the way things ended, but if Carson hadn't broken things off, I would have. And not because of what his father did. I loved Carson. I just wasn't in love with him."

"Oh."

"Aren't you going to ask me why I got engaged to someone I wasn't in love with?"

"No." He reached out and touched her hand. "You made the best decision you could at the time. If anyone understands that, it's me."

She pulled a few blades of grass, her eyes down. "Do you ever wonder what would have happened if you hadn't left? Or if you had come home sooner?"

"No. I have no doubt that Rivers would have killed me. He'd already killed someone. One more person wouldn't have made a difference." He blew out a breath.

"As for coming home while he was still alive…he could have killed all of you. That's a chance I wasn't willing to take."

She nodded.

"But as Elias wisely put it, we'll have to leave the past behind us and make the best of the present."

A strong wind blew and the temperature dropped several degrees. Donovan looked up. The sunny, blue sky had been replaced with a gray one. While he'd been entranced by Raven, a storm had blown in. Judging by the darkening sky, it was clearly going to be a bad one. They scrambled to their feet and began gathering the remnants of their lunch.

The wind blew again, carrying with it paper plates and plastic forks. "Leave it."

Raven nodded and balled up the quilt and shoved it into her saddlebag. "Elias. Let's go."

He raced over. "This is some crazy storm. Will the horses be okay to ride?"

"Yes."

Donovan looked at Raven. "Can Elias handle this? Maybe we should just wait it out."

"He's good. Trust me. It shouldn't take us long to get down from here."

Donovan nodded and swung onto his horse. "You lead. I'll go last, just in case."

Raven directed her horse down the decline. Elias followed. After watching for several tense minutes, Donovan relaxed a bit. Elias was every bit as skilled as Raven claimed. But then, the Reynolds raised horses. No doubt Elias had been on horseback from the time he could sit up.

They reached the bottom of the hill just as the rain

began to fall. It started slowly but, within a minute, big, fat drops were falling. The rain was steady, but fortunately not so heavy that it made it hard to see. They were at least an hour away from the house and Donovan hoped the weather wouldn't get much worse. Luckily there wasn't any lightning or thunder so there was less chance of the horses spooking.

By the time they reached the stable, they were soaked. Donovan dismounted and opened the stable doors and Raven and Elias rode inside. Once they were in the grooming area, they removed the saddles and blankets. Donovan was pleased to see that Elias didn't balk or complain about being wet. Instead he began to carefully yet quickly dry his horse. Once the horses were dried and brushed with their hooves cleaned, they gave them water and food and led them to open stalls.

"I'll clean up here," Donovan said, heading back to the grooming area.

"It'll be faster if we work together," Elias said.

Donovan was so proud of his son he could only nod. A good rancher always finished the job.

When they were done, they went inside the house, took off their wet boots and stepped barefoot into the kitchen. A note was taped to the refrigerator. Donovan's parents had accepted a dinner invitation from a neighbor. He nearly cheered. His parents were starting to live again.

"It looks like it's just us. Mom and Dad are out for the evening."

"That's good," Raven said softly. "They need to start getting out again. I don't think they left the house together more than ten times while you were away. I always thought they wanted someone to be here in case you called or came home."

"This is the first time they've left since I've been back. It's as if they expect me to disappear again." He sighed heavily as it hit him once more what his disappearance had done to his parents. The unending terror of not knowing where he was and what he might be enduring. There was no way he could change any of that so he made sure to be extra patient with them now. Hopefully having him around would help them to recover because although he loved them, he wanted to build his own home where Elias could visit him. Not only that, he wanted to fall in love again and get married.

When he was younger, Donovan and his parents had talked about him finding a spot on the ranch where he could build his own house. Since he'd been back, he'd been giving the idea a lot of consideration.

Elias sneezed. They all needed dry clothes. Raven was about the same size as his mother, but Donovan didn't feel comfortable offering his mother's belongings. "Come on. Let's get something for you to wear."

Raven and Elias followed Donovan through the house and to his room.

"Wow," Elias and Raven said at the same time. But while Elias's voice was filled with awe, Raven's voice sounded shocked.

"This is so cool," Elias said, racing to a shelf where Donovan's old superhero memorabilia was stored. He picked up a Black Panther comic and started to read it. Apparently having drenched clothing plastered to his body didn't bother the kid a bit.

"Your parents didn't change a thing."

"No. They wanted me to feel comfortable when I got back."

"Do you?"

"Not even a little bit. It felt familiar that first night, in a weird sort of way. Now it's a reminder of how tightly my parents were holding on to whatever piece of me they could. But I'm not nineteen anymore. I'm doing my best to help them see that." He winced. "My mother keeps trying to make my bed for me."

"Well, they did go out tonight. That's progress."

"Yeah. Hopefully they won't regress."

He grabbed three T-shirts from his drawer, tossing one to Elias and handing one to Raven, then dug out three pairs of basketball shorts, as well. The clothes would be too big for them, but they would do while their jeans were in the dryer. Elias continued reading until Raven prodded him to take off his wet shirt. Sighing, the boy put the book on the desk and tried to keep reading while grabbing the bottom of his wet shirt and pulling it over his head.

Donovan pulled off his shirt and used it to dry his chest before putting on the dry one. When he looked up, Raven was staring at him. There was definitely some heat in her eyes. But then she blinked and it was gone so fast he was sure any desire he thought he'd seen was a figment of his imagination. Perhaps he was just seeing in her eyes a reflection of the longing he felt for her.

"I need a little more privacy than you two."

"I don't mind." Donovan winked.

"Yeah, well I do. I'll be in the bathroom."

Donovan watched as she walked away then turned his attention to his son.

* * *

Raven closed the bathroom door and leaned against it. *Whew.* What was she doing staring at Donovan like that? True, his chest was perfectly sculpted from years of hard work and his abs were incredibly well defined, but even so, it wasn't as if she'd never seen a man's body before. In fact, she'd actually seen his body on more than one occasion. Of course the last time she'd seen it, he'd been nineteen. He'd been well-built back then, but his body had not looked remotely like it did now. He'd definitely put on some weight, all of it lean muscles.

Speaking of putting on weight. As she pulled off her wet shirt, she looked at herself in the mirror. She'd put on a few pounds in the past ten years. She was curvier than she'd been when he'd last seen her. Having a baby changed a woman's body. Not that she felt bad about hers. Being pregnant with their son was worth the extra seven pounds she now carried.

She pulled on Donovan's shirt and shorts and was struck by the intimacy of wearing clothes that belonged to him. She inhaled deeply in an attempt to surround herself with his personal scent. Instead she only smelled laundry detergent and fabric softener. That was probably for the best. Breathing in his scent every second would make it hard to maintain her balance around him. Not only that, it would make it harder for her to keep their relationship in the present and not drift back into the past when they were in love. That time had been wonderful, but she needed to stay grounded in the here and now.

The rain had really done a number on her hair. She didn't have a comb with her, so she dragged her fingers through it in an attempt to get the tangles out. When she'd done the best she could, she grabbed her shirt and went back to Donovan's room.

He'd taken out a box of his old comics and he and Elias were sprawled on the floor, sorting through them. As far back as Raven could remember, Donovan had loved comics and always spent his allowance on the latest. He's also added secondhand books to his collection, which had to number in the thousands. She'd never understood the attraction, but to each his own.

Elias had discovered superheroes when he was five and he'd been a fan ever since. Could a love of a hobby be inherited? She didn't know, but looking at the two of them together, it was clear that they shared more than a hobby.

Elias looked like Donovan had at the same age. Donovan had been tall and skinny at nine, the same as their son. They had the same almond-shaped, light gray eyes and the same stubborn chin. And that one dimple that flashed when they smiled. It was easy to project what Elias would look like in twenty years.

Donovan and Elias were enjoying themselves and, rather than disturb them, she leaned against the wall and soaked in the moment. She'd always known Elias needed a man in his life. Her father did his best, but he wasn't able to keep up with an energetic boy. That was part of the reason she'd agreed to marry Carson. He was good to her son and was a positive influence. Carson and Elias had gotten along well, but when she'd told Elias that she and Carson weren't going to get married, he'd only shrugged and said okay. If he missed Carson, he kept it to himself. But then Donovan had come on the scene at the same time and he'd filled any void that Carson left.

Or maybe it was actually the other way around. Perhaps Carson had been a stand-in for Donovan. Now that Donovan had returned, there was no longer a place for Carson in her and Elias's life. She sighed. That sounded terrible and she felt guilty for entertaining the idea. Carson deserved better than that.

"What's wrong?"

"Nothing. I was just thinking."

Donovan stacked up the comics and returned them to the cardboard box. Elias had a three-inch pile beside him. He gathered them in his arms and stood.

"Thanks for letting me borrow these. I'll bring them back as soon as I finish reading them."

"Take as much time as you need. When you finish with those, I have plenty more for you to read."

Donovan returned the box to the closet. Raven saw several more identical boxes that she knew held the rest of his collection. In that moment she was so glad Lena and Mario hadn't tossed out any of Donovan's belongings.

Donovan closed the door and looked at her. "Do you have time or do you need to get back right away?"

Raven thought of the work she'd left undone. She'd already put herself behind with the horseback ride and the extended lunch. She'd be working through the night at this rate. "We've got time."

"Great."

They tossed their wet clothes into the dryer on the way to the family room. Elias immediately hopped into a chair by the windows and opened a comic book. Donovan and Raven sat together on the couch. Despite telling herself that she shouldn't get caught up in a fantasy and suddenly pretend they were a happy family spending a rainy afternoon together, she couldn't deny that the idea held appeal. But she knew that if they got together, and that was a big if, it would have to happen later. He needed to get his feet back under him and she needed to be certain of how she felt. That could take months.

Neither she nor Donovan spoke. Instead they sat and watched the rain fall and listened to the pitter-patter of drops hitting the windows. Eventually the rain slowed and finally stopped. The sky lightened and the sun began to peek through the dissipating clouds. A rainbow appeared in the distance.

"I guess that's a sign that it's time for us to hit the road," Raven said, standing. "Come on, Elias. Our clothes are dry. It's time to get home."

"We need to talk," Donovan said. "Can I call you later?"

She shook her head. "I have a lot of work to finish tonight. One of Elias's friends is having a sleepover birthday party tomorrow so he won't be around to overhear. Maybe we can talk then."

"Sounds good."

Raven felt a bit sad to leave Donovan's house. It had felt good to be around him. But since they shared a son, she knew they would spend more time together.

But could they share more than a son?

Chapter Twelve

Raven checked her appearance in the mirror and then frowned. When did she turn into one of those women who spent hours getting ready for a simple date? When Donovan had called her this morning and suggested that they meet in person, she'd invited him over for dinner. He'd liked the idea of sharing a meal, but said he'd rather take her out. In a moment of weakness she'd said yes. Then she'd spent the rest of the day mentally choosing and then discarding every outfit in her closet. She'd even considered driving to town and buying a new outfit before she tossed the idea aside. She didn't have hours to waste. Besides she had several perfectly good dresses hanging in her closet.

This was a new development for her. She hadn't fretted about her clothes or accessories as a teenager. But then, her mother had always helped her select clothes when they went shopping. Although, like most female ranchers, she wore jeans most of the time, Marilyn had great fashion sense.

Unfortunately, Raven hadn't inherited her mother's sense of style. She'd never been interested in clothes. Raven was more like her father, who wore whatever clean shirt he grabbed from his drawer. Her clothes hadn't mattered when she was dating Carson. Oh, she'd always taken care to look her best, she just hadn't worried about her appearance like she was now.

And why was she so worried anyway? It wasn't as if she and Donovan were in love or anything close to it. This dinner wasn't part of some great plan Donovan had to woo her. They were meeting to discuss their son.

Donovan and Elias had many things in common and were growing close. Their relationship was progressing much more quickly than Raven had expected it to. Though she hated the idea of sharing custody of her son, she knew it was the right thing to do. They deserved the opportunity to establish a true father and son relationship. But first she and Donovan needed to come up with a way to tell Elias that Donovan was his father.

"You look nice," her mother said as Raven came downstairs to wait for Donovan. She'd settled on a blue print dress that she'd worn to Jericho and Camille's wedding. She'd received lots of compliments that day and she felt confident wearing it.

"What's the occasion?" her father asked.

"Donovan and I are going to dinner."

Her mother frowned. "I don't understand your attraction to that man."

"Marilyn," her father chided. "Raven is a grown woman, old enough to make her own decisions. Besides, I like Donovan. Always have."

"Thanks, Dad."

"I'm just saying that after the way he treated you, leaving you pregnant and alone, then staying away for ten years, you'd be smarter than to let him back into your life."

"It's my life. And you don't have all the facts." She could tell her mother about Karl Rivers, but loyalty to Carson kept her silent. She'd promised she wouldn't tell anyone about what his father had done and she wouldn't.

"I have all the facts I need. Poor Lena worried herself sick over that boy. Then he just waltzes back in like nothing happened. I understand why she let him back into her life. A mother never stops loving her child. But you…" Marilyn shook her head in disgust. "I raised you to be smarter than this."

Raven picked up her shawl and purse. "I think I'll wait for Donovan outside. I don't know when I'll be back, so don't wait up for me."

"Have a good time," her father called.

Her mother just grunted.

It was definitely time to think about getting her own place. Raven loved her parents and appreciated all the help they'd given her with Elias, but she was ready to be on her own. She and Elias both loved living on the ranch, but maybe it was time to move to Sweet Briar. He could spend more time with his friends and she could put her accounting degree to work for other clients. She would still keep books for the ranch, of course. She would just do it remotely.

But moving would make it more difficult for Donovan to spend time with Elias. Right now they lived minutes apart and could get together on the spur of the moment. Sweet Briar was an hour away. She blew out a breath. She couldn't think only of herself and what she wanted. Donovan had a stake in her decision so she needed to consult him, as well.

She saw his truck coming up the driveway and stood. The red paint shone. He must have spent hours washing and waxing it. When he got out of the truck and came to the stairs, she was glad she'd taken extra time with her appearance. He was wearing a charcoal-gray suit with a subtly striped shirt. He'd forgone a tie and the shirt was open at the collar. *Yowza.* That man certainly knew how to take a girl's breath away.

He handed her a small, gaily wrapped box. After the briefest hesitation, he kissed her cheek. The scent of his cologne wrapped around her like a lover's embrace.

"You look fabulous," Donovan said.

"Thanks. I was just thinking the same about you."

"After we talked, I realized my wardrobe was sadly lacking, so I went to town and bought this suit."

Raven thanked her lucky stars that she hadn't given in to the urge to go shopping in town. It would have been too embarrassing to run into Donovan and explain why she was getting something new for tonight.

"It's great."

He nodded. "Aren't you going to open your gift?"

"You didn't have to get me anything." Her heart skipped several beats as she untied the thin ribbon and tore away the paper. She opened the box and looked inside. "A bracelet."

"I found a bracelet I'd gotten for you in my drawer last night. It was a present for your birthday, but I never got a chance to give it to you. It looked a little worse for wear, so I bought you this one instead. Happy belated birthday."

"Thanks." Her eyes filled with tears and she quickly blinked them away. She held out her wrist and allowed Donovan to slip on the bracelet. It was silver and black with a hammered heart charm. It was the most beautiful piece of jewelry she'd ever seen and it was definitely the most elegant piece she'd ever owned. "I love it."

"I'm glad. Ready to go?"

She nodded.

He held out his arm and she slipped her hand over his biceps, feeling the strength there.

After he helped her into his truck, he climbed in beside her, started the engine and turned on the radio. "What kind of music do you listen to now?"

"Any kind. After years of Raffi, Jim Gill and Charlotte Diamond played on repeat, I'm happy with whatever comes on the radio."

"Who are they? I've never heard of any of them."

"They sing children songs and were Elias's favorite musicians when he was little. I swear he spent every waking hour either listening to one of them or singing one of their songs. It's been a couple of years since we played them on a regular rotation, but I swear I can still hear those songs in my head." She pretended to shiver.

Donovan laughed but it sounded sad. No doubt he was thinking about all that he'd missed. She wouldn't offer some lame platitude that wouldn't comfort him. Nor would she lie and tell him that what he'd missed hadn't been wonderful because it had been. Raising Elias had been the single most important thing she'd done in her life. She wouldn't insult Donovan by pretending he hadn't missed out on one of life's greatest blessings. But she could let him know there was still more to experience.

"Even though Elias has outgrown his children's music phase, his taste in music is eclectic. In school they studied music from around the world to help them learn respect for other cultures. He discovered the didgeridoo and fell in love with the sound and wanted to learn how to play. He was disappointed when I told him I wasn't going to buy him one, so he decided that opera was his new favorite kind of music. After all, he didn't need me to buy him a voice. He walked around the house singing Pavarotti as loud as he could. He can't carry a tune in a basket. I just think he was doing it out of revenge. Still, if you like, I can get him to sing *O Sole Mio* or *Nessun Dorma* for you."

This time Donovan's laughter was completely happy. "I might take you up on that."

They chatted and laughed as they drove to town. Although Raven didn't come to Sweet Briar often, she loved visiting. The town had grown these past few years, bringing in new businesses and new people. Several women had made overtures of friendship, inviting her to lunch or girls' night out, but she'd never accepted. She regretted that and vowed that next time she would say yes.

"I got a reservation at Heaven on Earth," Donovan said as he parked the truck.

"Really? How'd you pull that off?"

"Jericho and the owner are good friends."

"You won't be disappointed. The food is fabulous."

As soon as they stepped inside, a hostess greeted them, checked for their reservation then led them to their table. Donovan pulled out Raven's chair and held it for her. The little courtesy made her smile. He removed his jacket and then sat across from her. A few seconds later a waitress appeared with their menus.

"I can't tell you the last time I've been in a nice restaurant," Donovan said.

"You didn't do a lot of dating?" Raven asked, trying not to sound as curious as she was. Just because he hadn't wanted to have a serious relationship didn't mean he'd become a monk. Plenty of women could have come in and out of his life over the past decade.

There was so much she didn't know about him. So much she wanted to know. Although she told herself she was only interested in Donovan because of the role he was about to play in Elias's life, she knew that wasn't true. She wanted to know more about the man he'd become because she was attracted to him again. At this rate it wouldn't be too hard for her to fall in love with him again. But did she really want that?

Donovan tried to focus on his menu long enough to select an entrée, but Raven wasn't making it easy. Her shawl had slipped from her bare shoulder, revealing soft skin that his hands ached to touch. The dress wasn't cut low but it revealed enough of her breasts to make him sweat. But as appealing as her body was, it was her face that kept him distracted. The light in her eyes when she spoke of their son. The smile on her face when she found something amusing. He could spend the night watching the play of expressions on her face and never get bored.

"I think I'll have the paella," Raven said, handing her menu to the waitress.

"That sounds good. Make it two."

"Very good. I'll be back with your drinks right away." The waitress smiled and walked away.

"So where were we?" Donovan asked.

"You were talking about how long it had been since you were in a nice restaurant."

"Right."

"You can't tell me there were no good restaurants in all of Texas."

"There were plenty. I just never felt compelled to visit one. After a while I made friends. Some of them were women, but none were the type I'd dress up to take out."

"Did you miss it? Dating and having someone you loved in your life?"

He exhaled. No small talk for them. Raven was going straight to the heart of the matter. "Sure. I don't know of a person who doesn't want to love and be loved in return. But I had pretty much resigned myself to that not happening for me. Not under those circumstances, and I didn't see those circumstances ever changing. I wanted a family, a wife, children, a home, but I didn't think I would ever have one. And it turns out that I had a son all along."

"Yes." Raven sipped her sweet tea. "I think we should tell Elias that you're his father. It's time."

Donovan's heart leaped. He'd been hoping she'd say that. But now that she'd actually said the words he felt weak. "When?"

"Sooner rather than later. Tomorrow?"

"How do you think he'll take it?"

Raven shrugged. "I don't know. I never spoke badly of you, so there's no reason he should have negative thoughts about you. And the two of you get along well, so…"

"Do you think he might want to spend time with me? Alone, I mean? Maybe even spend a night once in a while?"

Raven looked away from him and nodded. Clearly she was torn.

"I'm not going to try to take him away from you. I just want him in my life. I want to listen to him as he tries to sing opera or yodel or whatever his next phase of music is. I think there's enough room in his life for both of us, don't you?"

"Of course."

She said the right words but Donovan wondered if she truly believed them. Was she worried about losing her son? Didn't she trust Donovan to keep his word? Or was she worried that he wouldn't be a good father? Whatever the issue, they would need to work it out. But that would only happen with time.

They changed the subject and told funny stories of their lives. Unlike their earlier conversation, they didn't talk at all about Elias. Donovan loved his son and was looking forward to having him in his life, but that relationship, while important, wouldn't be enough to sustain Donovan emotionally. He wanted a woman to share his life. Raven had been his one true love when they were younger. Maybe she still was. But the only way to know if any of the love they'd shared remained was to spend time getting to know each other again.

They lingered over coffee and dessert. After paying the bill and tipping the waitress, they went outside. The night was pleasant and Donovan wasn't ready for it to end. "You up for a walk on the beach?"

"I'd love that."

Donovan took one look at Raven's high heels and decided to drive the short distance. Once he'd parked, they walked across the paved path to the sand. Without speaking, they each removed their shoes. He was wearing socks so he took them off, as well. They tucked their shoes under a bench and he hoped like heck they'd be there when he and Raven returned. He'd bought those shoes today and hadn't even broken them in yet. Taking her hand, he led her to the water's edge. The moon was high in the midnight-blue sky and cast its glow on the ocean. He sighed. "I missed this so much."

"Not many beaches in the middle of Texas?"

"Not that I saw." He'd been talking about missing holding her hand. Missing talking for hours and not running out of things to say. Missing being together whether on a beach or on the ranch. He'd missed her.

"Now that you're back, I bet you'll want to make up for lost time."

"If only that was possible." He stopped in his tracks and turned so they were facing each other. "I missed you, Raven. Every day. Every night."

"I missed you, too."

He reached out and touched her cheek. Her skin was unbearably soft. When she leaned her face into his hand, he lowered his head and brushed his lips against hers. Their lips touched and tingles ran down his spine. He pulled back and she grabbed his shirt, bringing him close to her again. She didn't have to tell him twice. He wrapped his arms around her waist and deepened the kiss.

It had been so long since he'd held her, but his body remembered everything about her. He remembered the taste of her. Her scent. Time and distance had separated them, but some memories could never be erased.

The waves lapped against the shore, covering their feet with warm water. He heard teenagers talking, their voices growing louder as they grew closer. Though he didn't want to stop kissing Raven, he pulled back then leaned his forehead against hers. Their breathing was labored and as their chests rose and fell, neither spoke.

He glanced over his shoulder. The teenagers were close now, so he stepped back and took Raven's hand and they began walking along the sand again. He wanted to take her into his arms once more, but knew that they each needed time to figure out what was going on between them. Before he made any type of commitment, he wanted to be sure that what he felt was real and not the residue of their past relationship. He wasn't sure how to distinguish between the desire and growing affection he felt for Raven now and the love he'd held on to for ten years. But he had to try.

Maybe Raven was experiencing similar confusion. After all, she'd been ready to marry another man a week ago. Now that her engagement was over, she might be lonely and longing for love. She might be trying to fill an empty place in her heart. He wouldn't blame her if that was the case. If anyone deserved to be loved and happy, it was Raven. Maybe, like him, she was trying to figure out what was real and what was memory. The best thing for both of them was to take their time.

"Come on," he said, turning and heading back to the entrance. "We'd better get going."

She sighed and leaned her head against his shoulder. "I know. It'll be morning before we know it."

They walked arm in arm to the car, not in any particular hurry to get there. They were quiet on the ride back to the ranch, listening to an oldies' station playing songs from when they were in high school. "The term 'old school' doesn't mean what it used to."

Raven laughed. "You can say that again."

When they reached Raven's house, Donovan parked and turned to look at her. "I had a great time tonight."

"So did I."

"So where do we go from here?"

"I don't know. I guess the best thing to do is to take it one step at a time. And the first step is to tell Elias you're his dad. No matter what, we're going to have to be friends."

"Deal." But friends didn't kiss like that, did they?

He helped her out of the truck and they walked to her front door. He resisted the urge to take her into his arms and kiss her like he wanted to. Instead he settled for a peck on the cheek. He waited until she'd unlocked the door and stepped inside before getting into his truck and heading home to his lonely bed.

Chapter Thirteen

Raven hummed as she ran the comb through her hair. He'd kissed her last night. She'd anticipated that moment since she'd seen him get out of his truck looking like a man who'd gone the extra mile to appeal to his date. She paused. No, the truth was she'd dreamed of that kiss from the moment she'd seen him standing on her porch last week.

The problem was that she was still trying to figure out whether their feelings were the real thing. Perhaps they were wondering what would have happened between them if the past ten years had played out differently. Whenever she thought of Donovan, the emotions of the past and the present got all twisted and she became confused, making thinking nearly impossible.

Annoyed with herself, she put down her comb and pulled her hair into a ponytail. She'd somehow managed to turn a wonderful recollection into a jumble of confusion and worry. She'd better get herself together before her father got back with Elias.

Her parents had been asleep when she'd gotten home, so she hadn't been able to tell them about her decision to tell Elias that Donovan was his father until this morning. As expected, her mother had been opposed to the idea. If her father had an opinion, he'd kept it to himself. Instead he'd offered to pick up Elias from his friend's house. They should be back in a few minutes. She expected Donovan to arrive at the same time.

She heard her father's truck in the driveway and went down the stairs and onto the porch to greet them. Donovan's truck pulled up behind them. Before her father could come to a complete stop, Elias jumped from the vehicle and stormed up the stairs. The look on his face was one of pure rage. His face was contorted and his eyes flashed like lightning.

"What's wrong?" she asked. She looked from her son to her father in search of an answer.

"Liar," Elias yelled. "You're a liar and I hate you."

Raven froze. Elias pushed past her and went into the house, letting the screen door slam behind him.

"What happened?" she asked her father, who was slowly climbing the stairs. Donovan was right behind him, concern etched on his face.

Her father shook his head and looked at her and then at Donovan. "He knows Donovan is his father."

"What?" Raven's knees weakened and she grabbed onto the banister for support. Donovan was there immediately, wrapping his arms around her waist and holding her up.

"How?" Donovan asked the question that was echoing through Raven's mind.

"We stopped by Polly Wants A Cookie to get some brownies and Cynthia Smith was there. It's no secret to the people around here that Donovan is Elias's father. Everyone knew you were dating when he vanished. Not to mention that Elias looks exactly like Donovan. Apparently she saw the three of you at the carnival and assumed Elias knew Donovan was his father. She said he must be glad his dad is back home."

"That old busybody," Raven muttered. "Why can't people just mind their own business?"

"She didn't mean any harm. She thought he knew."

Raven expelled a breath. "I understand. Not that it matters. What's done is done. Now I have to try to clean up this mess."

"Not you," Donovan said. "We. We have to straighten this out."

"Elias is upset," Raven said. "It might be best if I talk to him."

"No. I'm his father. I'm not going to step aside and let you shut me out. If there's a problem, we need to handle it together."

"That's not what I'm doing."

Raven's father raised his hands and backed up. "I'm going to let the two of you work this out. But I suggest you come to a decision soon. Elias is waiting."

After her father went inside, Raven turned to Donovan. "I'm not trying to shut you out. I just think that it would be best if I handled it alone. He may know that you're his biological father, but you don't have that type of relationship with him."

"And I never will if you keep pushing me aside. We need to start somewhere. We know better than anyone that we don't get to choose what happens to us. We planned to tell him today, but someone else beat us to the punch. The only thing we can do now is deal with it. I'm ready to do that. Are you willing to let me be a real part of his life or are you going to keep trying to call all the shots?"

Raven had thought she was prepared for how different things would be once Elias knew Donovan was his father. She wasn't. Naturally it had occurred to her that she wouldn't be in control all the time because she wouldn't always be around. Elias and Donovan would spend time alone. But she'd thought she would have final say in Elias's life. If she and Donovan disagreed, she'd have the last word. She'd been mistaken. Donovan wasn't willing to take a back seat. Even now, when she knew best, he was unwilling to let her take the lead.

"I think it's best if I handle this alone." She'd raised Elias for nine years and knew how to reach him. He was her son after all.

"He's my son, too."

"I know that. I just think it's a mistake for us both to talk to him. It will look like we're ganging up on him."

"We're presenting a unified front. Besides, you're kidding yourself if you think he won't have questions for me. Only I can answer them."

Raven swallowed her retort. Going back and forth wouldn't solve the problem. And clearly they weren't going to agree. "Okay. You win. Let's go."

Her heart grew heavier as they climbed the stairs to Elias's room. Though she didn't condone the way Elias had behaved, she understood his anger. One of the promises she'd made to herself and to Elias was that she'd never lie to him. She had broken that promise. She knew she had the very best reason for not revealing Donovan's identity before now, but that didn't change the situation.

She knocked on Elias's closed door.

"Go away."

"You really don't think I'm going to do that, do you?" Raven turned the knob and stepped inside, Donovan right behind her. Elias was staring out the window at the backyard. He had a view of the stable and corral though she doubted he was seeing either one of them right now.

"I don't want to talk to you," Elias said, turning to face them. His eyes flashed. She didn't think she'd ever seen him this upset. But underneath the anger she saw sadness and pain so deep it made her heart ache for him.

"Then listen while I talk to you."

"Why? You're only going to lie to me. You're just a big fat liar."

Donovan stepped around Raven and was in Elias's face so fast he might have actually had superpowers. Donovan leaned down until his face was even with Elias's. Their angry gray eyes collided. When Donovan spoke, his voice was surprisingly quiet yet firm. "You can be as angry at me as you want. You can even be angry at your mother, although she's not to blame for any of this. But what you won't do is be disrespectful to your mother. Not now. Not ever. Do you hear me?"

"Donovan, it's okay—" Raven began.

Donovan raised a hand to silence her, but his eyes never left their son's face.

"I asked you a question. Do you understand?"

Elias lifted his chin defiantly and glared at Donovan. Raven worried how Donovan would feel if Elias didn't respond. Their relationship was new and tenuous. She didn't want it to be ruined. But if she interrupted, that would only weaken Donovan's position. After a long moment Elias looked away. "Yes."

"Good."

Raven stepped closer. "We were going to tell you today when you got home."

Elias sneered. "You're only saying that because you got caught in your lie. If Mrs. Smith didn't tell me, I would never have known the truth. You and Donovan would have kept on pretending that you were just friends. Donovan would have kept pretending that he was my friend."

Elias spit out Donovan's name as if it tasted nasty on his tongue.

"And everyone in the bakery heard. I bet all of my friends know that Donovan is my so-called father now. Everybody knows he disappeared all those years ago and never came back to see me. Everybody knows he's pretending to be my friend."

"We were going to tell you," Raven repeated. "That's why Donovan is here today. He knew you went to that sleepover and that your grandfather had gone to pick you up."

Elias crossed his arms over his chest. "I don't believe you. I'll never believe anything you say again."

Raven flinched. "I'm sorry to hear that."

"Don't blame your mother. She was caught off guard when I returned. She was only trying to protect you. She hadn't seen me in ten years and didn't know what kind of man I was. It was important for her to get to know me again before she told you who I was. Your mother only wanted to make sure I didn't hurt you."

Elias grunted but he was listening.

"And, for the record, I never pretended to be your friend. I am your friend."

"I thought you were supposed to be my father."

"I can be both."

"No thanks. I don't need you to be either. I have friends. Real friends who don't lie to me. And I don't need a father. And my mom doesn't need you to be her boyfriend. She doesn't need you to hold her hand and try to kiss her. We were fine without you." His voice trembled and tears began to run down his cheeks. "Why don't you go back where you were and stay there this time? We don't want you here."

Donovan stiffened. Elias's words hit him like a closed fist. His face was drawn and he looked tired. Raven reached out to him, but he dodged her hand. She'd known things weren't going to go well. Elias was too hurt to have a rational discussion. He felt as if she and Donovan had not only betrayed him—in his mind they'd played him for a fool. He was bound to lash out. If only Donovan had listened, she could have explained things to Elias without Donovan getting hurt.

"I'll leave then." Donovan took two steps and she followed him.

"Donovan, he just needs time."

"Of course." He said the only words he could say under the circumstances, but Raven could see beneath them to the hurt he couldn't quite mask. It was as if all of his dreams had turned to ashes.

"Wait," Elias said, giving her hope. Then he walked to his desk and picked up the stack of comics he'd borrowed. Raven knew he hadn't read all of them. "I don't want these anymore."

Donovan hesitated then took the comic books. The

pain radiating from him was so strong it could have knocked her over. Donovan slowly walked out of the room, closing the door behind him. Until Raven heard his footsteps grow fainter, she held on to hope that Elias would relent and tell his father not to go. That hope died a hard death. Elias was too hurt and angry to back down now.

"We were going to tell you," Raven repeated when she and Elias were alone.

"But you didn't." Elias looked at Raven. He'd stopped crying and his face looked fierce. "I don't ever want to see him again. If you try and make me, I'll run away."

"Don't say things you might regret."

"I'm not. I mean it. I hate him."

Raven sighed. How had this turned into such a mess? More importantly, how was she going to fix it? Because although Elias didn't want to admit it, he needed Donovan in his life. And so did she.

Donovan leaned his head against the tree trunk and closed his eyes. Two days had passed since his son had turned his back on him. He'd held out hope that once Elias had calmed down he'd want to talk. Donovan had hoped Elias would at least hear him out, but that hadn't been the case. Elias didn't trust him. They hadn't had enough time to build a relationship that could withstand a test like this. And as Elias had pointed out, he'd lived without a father for nine years. He didn't need Donovan.

As disappointed as he was not to hear from his son, he was even more hurt that he hadn't heard from Raven. She'd been angry at him initially and hadn't wanted to let him become a part of Elias's life, but he'd thought she'd come around. Once she knew why he'd stayed away, she'd warmed up to him. They'd been making progress in their relationship. He'd actually believed they were becoming friends. And a part of him thought that, given enough time, they might have become even more than that.

Even when he'd had little to no hope that he'd ever see Raven again, part of him had still been in love with her. She'd won his heart when they were young and neither time nor distance had changed that. Perhaps he'd been holding on to her because she was a link to the life he'd left behind. But it hadn't felt that way. When they were together, the feelings he felt for her were new. Fresh. He'd been falling in love with her again. Now he wondered if he'd imagined it all.

If her silence was anything to go by, the feelings were definitely one-sided. Maybe she was glad to have Donovan out of her life and was using Elias's anger as a reason to keep him away. Obviously she hadn't held on to her feelings the way he'd held on to his. And why should she have? Even if she'd hoped he was still alive, she couldn't keep living in the past. Not when she had a child to raise. It would be impossible to hold on to the past and move forward at the same time.

Carson Rivers was proof that she'd moved on. She'd been planning on marrying the other man. Carson had been the one to end it, not Raven. For all Donovan knew, she could be longing for her former fiancé. And even if she wasn't, it didn't mean that she was emotionally ready to fall in love with someone else. For all Donovan knew, he was a rebound guy. Or maybe Raven had spent time with him to avoid dealing with her feelings about her broken engagement. He didn't know because they'd never talked about their feelings. Everything was speculation on his part.

One thing he knew for sure. He wasn't giving up on his son. He didn't know if Raven was encouraging Elias to forgive him for being absent for all of his life or if she was doing the opposite. He hoped Raven was on his side, but whether she was or not, he was determined to win back his son. He'd lost too much time. He wasn't going to sit back and lose any more.

Chapter Fourteen

Raven stared out at the darkening sky and sighed. She missed Donovan. Two long days had passed since she'd seen him. The expression on his face would stay with her for the rest of her life. He'd looked positively wrecked. No matter how hard she tried not to, she could see him wilt as if each word of Elias's rejection packed the power of a comic book villain's punch.

Raven knew that Elias hadn't meant what he'd said. That had been his pain talking. She'd felt the same way when Donovan had showed up out of the blue, so she understood where Elias was coming from. But she also knew that the longer she allowed him to hold on to his anger, the better chance it had of festering and becoming an insurmountable obstacle in his life.

Donovan and Elias had the potential to have a great relationship. Despite the fact that Elias hadn't grown up around Donovan, he had some of his behaviors. There were times when he had an expression on his face that so resembled Donovan's it took her breath away.

Part of her wondered if she wasn't at least partially to blame for the rift. After all, she was the one who'd insisted that Donovan keep his identity a secret from Elias. She was the one who hadn't believed in him or trusted his motives. True, she had only been trying to protect her son, but if she had allowed him to tell Elias the truth when Donovan first came back, they wouldn't be in this predicament now. Maybe Elias and Donovan would be well on their way to establishing a strong father and son relationship.

And maybe she and Donovan would be continuing to develop their relationship. Things had been going so well. She'd been so confused lately. Maybe this weekend would help clarify her feelings. She knew what it felt like to be in love as a teenager. She had no idea what it felt like as an adult. Perhaps after this weekend she would know what she felt.

She'd already made a huge mistake with Carson. There was no way she was going to make a similar mistake with Donovan. She needed to be sure of her feelings before she took one more step in his direction. It would be great to have time alone to ponder the depths of her feelings, but that wasn't possible. She had to get Donovan and Elias back on track. There was no way Elias was going to spend time with Donovan on his own, so she would have to be there, too. She already had a plan.

The event she had in mind wasn't going to be an easy one for her to navigate. Joni Danielson, director of the Sweet Briar youth center, had been granted permission by Jericho and Camille Jones to have a family campout on his land. Jericho and Camille had been hosting children who lived in town on day trips where the kids rode horses and experienced life on a working ranch. From everything Raven heard, the children enjoyed the experience. This weekend wasn't limited to children nor was it strictly for people who lived in town. In fact, ranchers and their children were encouraged to attend.

When Raven had first read the flier announcing the event, she'd thought it an interesting idea but hadn't given it a second thought. But that was before things had gone to hell in the proverbial handbasket. Now she had no choice but to take drastic action. Returning to her desk, she turned on her computer and completed the online registration form, signing them up for the weekend adventure. Now she just needed to tell Donovan and Elias the three of them would not only be attending the camp but they would be participating in all of the activities as a family.

Once she'd paid the fee, Raven's heart sped up at the prospect of sharing a tent with Donovan. For a moment she wondered if her interest in the weekend together was strictly because she wanted Donovan and Elias to rebuild their relationship. Or was it because she hoped to reignite the fire between her and Donovan? Regardless of her motives, it was done. The chips were going to fall wherever they landed. She just hoped that no matter what happened, her heart would be able to take it.

She was about to pick up the phone to tell Donovan what she'd done when she hesitated. Had she just made a huge mistake? After all, it had been a pretty big assumption on her part. He might not want to spend the entire weekend with them. Maybe he had ideas of his own about how to get things straightened out. Would he think she was trying to control everything?

The phone rang and she looked at the screen. Donovan. Her heart skipped a beat and for a moment it was difficult to breathe. There was no pretending that she was suddenly excited to talk to him because of Elias. She was thrilled simply because she wanted to talk to him. She missed him. Missed hearing his voice. Missed seeing his face. And despite what Elias believed, she wanted Donovan to kiss her and hold her hand.

"Donovan," she said, picking up. There was a pause as if he hadn't expected that greeting.

"Raven, I need to talk to you."

"I was about to call you."

"Really?"

The doubt in his voice pierced her heart. Why was everything so hard between them?

"Yes. But clearly you don't believe me. Why?"

"Oh, I don't know. Maybe because two days have passed and I haven't heard a word from you. I have no idea what's going on with my son."

"He's angry. You know that. Surely you didn't think it would blow over that quickly, did you?"

"I guess I hadn't expected him to hold a grudge this long. But maybe he's had help."

Her excitement about her plan to get Donovan and Elias together fizzled and she grew indignant. She tried to put herself in his shoes, but she was tired of having to deal with everyone's attitude with a smile. She was sick of being the one who had to understand how everyone else felt while no one had to consider how she felt. And she was too annoyed to watch what she said or how she said it. "What are you accusing me of?"

"You didn't want me in Elias's life in the first place. Maybe this is your way of keeping me on the outside and having him all to yourself."

"Your memory is flawed. I didn't know about you in the first place. You were gone. When you returned, there was no way in hell I was going to let you be alone with my child. But I didn't keep you from him. And, lest you forget, you agreed that we wouldn't tell him who you were right away. It might have been a mistake, but it was our mistake, not mine."

Donovan sighed. "You're right. I'm just frustrated. I'm in the dark and I don't know what's going on. I know it's not your fault that I missed so much of his life."

"Sure," she scoffed. "You say one thing and then do another. I thought we were becoming friends and that we were working toward a common goal."

"We were. We are."

He didn't say more, but then nothing he said would change the fact that he didn't trust her. And no matter how attracted she was to him, they couldn't have anything real without trust.

She let the subject drop and moved on to what she'd planned to tell him. He listened without interrupting her. When she was finished, he still didn't speak.

"Well?" she prompted. "If you don't want to do it, just say so."

"No. I mean yes. That sounds like a great idea."

"You could be a little more enthused."

"I am. I feel so much worse for accusing you of working against me. I should have known you wouldn't sabotage my relationship with Elias."

"But you didn't." And his lack of faith was a knife to her heart.

"I'm sorry."

"We don't know each other very well. Hopefully in time we'll be able to give each other the benefit of the doubt before jumping to conclusions."

"I hope so."

After discussing the particulars, they said good-night and ended the conversation. Though he'd apologized for not trusting her, his lack of faith in her left Raven with an empty feeling in her heart. Where she used to smile as she fell asleep since he'd been back, tonight two tears slid down her cheeks as she closed her eyes. How many times did her heart have to break before she faced the truth? Their love was gone. If there was a way to get it back, she didn't know it.

Donovan's heart thudded in his chest as he pulled up to Raven's driveway and cut the engine of his truck. He was still trying to wrap his head around the fact that he was going to spend the weekend with Raven and Elias. He felt so ashamed when he recalled accusing Raven of being delighted to have him out of their lives when she'd been working out a way to help him and Elias reconcile. Even though he had apologized, Donovan knew he'd done irreparable damage to their relationship. Words alone wouldn't undo the damage he'd done. The problem was, he didn't know how to make things better. It was possible that there was nothing he could do. Sometimes there was no fixing things no matter how much you wish you could.

He couldn't count the number of times he wished he had stayed with Raven and listened to what she'd had to tell him. How badly he wished he'd never encountered Karl Rivers that night. He'd spent years wishing for the power to go back in time and erase the event that had altered his life. But there had been no going back and making different moves. Just as there was no changing this. He'd said what he'd said. But since he couldn't change the past, he would make sure not to repeat his mistake in the future. First he would rebuild his relationship with his son then he'd work on repairing his relationship with Raven. He knew he couldn't have one without the other. Not that he wanted Elias without Raven. He wanted both.

Raven had suggested that he wait outside. He checked his watch. He was on time. Maybe Elias was giving her a hard time about Donovan coming this weekend. Even though it was difficult, Donovan decided to sit back and let Raven take the lead. Now that some time had passed, he could see he'd been wrong to insist on going with her to talk to Elias that day. She knew Elias better than he did. Maybe she would have been able to get through to him if Donovan hadn't been standing right there.

Just when he was beginning to wonder if Elias had refused to come, the front door opened and he stomped down the stairs. He was dragging a backpack in one hand and a sleeping bag in the other. His gear bumped on each step as he descended, but he didn't seem to notice or care. When he reached Donovan, he glared at him. Donovan had his work cut out for him. He decided on the spot that if Elias didn't want to talk, he wasn't going to force him. They had time.

Elias might be angry now and acting out, but he was basically a good kid. Donovan didn't think he would be able to stay angry and rude for long. Raven had raised him too well for that. Besides, it didn't seem to be his true nature.

Donovan followed Elias's lead and didn't speak, either. He stood aside as Elias tossed his gear in the truck bed, slamming his stuff on top of the tent Donovan had bought especially for the occasion.

Raven stepped outside and Donovan immediately raced up the stairs to help her with her bags. Dressed in a simple, white-cotton blouse that made her brown skin glow and black jeans that hugged her hips, she was the sexiest woman he'd seen in his life. With her thick hair pulled into a ponytail on top of her head, she looked exactly as she had at nineteen.

"Let me take this for you," he said, slipping her backpack from her slender shoulder. As he leaned over, her sweet scent encircled him and his pulse sped up.

"Thanks." She smiled and for a brief moment he wished it was just going to be the two of them alone in the tent. But then again, that might further complicate their relationship. He was going to have to find a way to keep his growing desire under control. Their hands brushed and his nerve endings seemed to catch fire. Deciding to turn down his lust was going to be easier to say than to do.

Donovan opened Raven's door before setting her gear in the truck bed beside his. Elias was already in the back seat. He grunted when Donovan started the engine, the first sound he'd made so far. Donovan took it as a sign that Elias was warming up to the idea of spending the weekend together.

As if reading Donovan's mind, Elias spoke, squashing that bit of hope. "I didn't want to come. The only reason I'm here is because Mom said I had to. But I want you to know that I still don't like you and I don't want you to be my friend or father."

Raven opened her mouth but Donovan touched her hand before she could speak. This wasn't something she could fix by telling Elias to behave. He and Elias were going to have to solve their problems on their own. Elias had stated where he stood and Donovan would do the same. "Noted. And I want you to know that I like you and I am your father. Nothing you say or do is going to change either thing."

Elias didn't have a reply to that, so he turned and stared out the window.

The organizers of the event had shared a list of items that were forbidden for the weekend. All electronics except cell phones for the adults were considered contraband and would be confiscated and held until Sunday afternoon. So Elias couldn't tune out Donovan by plugging in earbuds. Donovan turned on the car radio to fill the silence, not feeling even a twinge of guilt about being able to listen to his music while Elias couldn't. Age had its privilege.

"So, how have you been?" Raven asked. He had a feeling she was trying to show Elias how to be polite. Donovan could have given an equally polite answer, but on the off chance she really wanted to know, he gave as sincere and revealing an answer as he could.

"Great. I've been thinking of changing our cattle operation. Before…" He glanced over his shoulder. Elias was listening even though he was trying hard to pretend that he wasn't, so Donovan moderated his answer. He didn't need to spell it out because Raven knew what he meant. "Dad and I had been talking about going completely organic. We'd done some investigating and were taking steps to get started. All of that sort of fell by the wayside. Now that I'm back, we're going to give it another go."

Her eyes lit up and she smiled at him. He loved her smile. It was like a rainbow after a storm: a reminder that no matter how much upheaval there was in life, good things still existed in the world. "I remember. You were so excited."

"I still am. I finally feel like I'm putting down roots again. It's like…"

"Coming home?"

"Yeah."

"I'm so glad. You've been back for a while, but you're finally making long-term decisions. It's proof that you know you belong here and that you're back to stay. You're putting the pieces of your life together."

Donovan nodded. Raven had been always been good at making sense of his feelings even when he couldn't articulate them clearly. Whenever he'd been struggling to make sense of conflicting ideas, she'd been able to help him separate his thoughts and emotions and come up with a coherent plan.

When they arrived at Jericho's ranch, he was surprised by the number of cars parked on the front lawn and the amount of people unloading their equipment.

"Hey, there's Bobby and Kenny," Elias exclaimed. "I didn't know they were coming."

Apparently the presence of two of his friends was enough to get him out of his funk. He opened his door and was about to go running off when Donovan stopped him. "Let's get our stuff and sign in first. Your friends are going to be here all weekend."

Elias changed direction and helped Donovan unload their gear while Raven signed them in. She returned shortly, carrying two sealed manila envelopes and a stack of papers. She handed Donovan and Elias their envelopes then leaned against his truck and continued to read her paperwork.

Elias tore open his envelope and pulled out a handful of papers. After a moment, Donovan did the same. The first page contained general information about the ranch. There was a map that showed where they would be camping. It looked to be about three miles from the main house, near a lake. Donovan recognized the area immediately. He and his closest friends had spent a lot of time on the Double J. They'd had some great times. That's what he wanted for Elias. Good friends and good times.

"This is going to be so much fun," Elias said to no one in particular.

"Do you think we can win any of the contests?" Donovan asked.

"Yeah. We're both strong and Mom sorta is."

"Hey." Raven poked him with her elbow. "I'm strong."

Donovan and Elias looked at each other and laughed. Then, as if realizing he was still supposed to be angry at Donovan, Elias frowned and picked up his backpack and sleeping bag. "We're supposed to meet in the back."

Donovan sighed as Elias walked away. Raven grabbed Donovan around the biceps and leaned her head against his shoulder. "Give him time. He likes you. It won't take long for him to remember that. Not to mention that it takes him far more effort to be angry than to just relax and be friends."

"I know you're right. I'm not discouraged. I've just got to be patient."

"Good." She gave his arm a gentle squeeze that did more to lift his spirits than her words then picked up her bags and followed Elias. Donovan watched the sway of her hips before picking up the remainder of their gear and following them.

Raven and Elias were standing near the side of the assembling group and Donovan joined them. He saw a few familiar faces and returned the smiles and waves. There were many people he didn't recognize, which only emphasized the fact that life here had continued without him. He didn't feel bitter now, though. Perhaps because as Raven said the pieces of his life were coming together.

A woman in her twenties stood in the middle of the semicircle and raised her hand, asking for attention. Everyone got quiet. "Thanks. For those of you who don't know me, I'm Joni Danielson and I'm the director of the Sweet Briar youth center. Welcome to our very first family camp. Hopefully this will become an annual event. Before I say anything more, I'd like to thank Jericho and Camille Jones for hosting us."

There was applause and cries of thank you from several of the adults. Jericho and Camille smiled and nodded. Donovan couldn't help but notice how happy his friend and his wife were. It was as if they were in a world of their own. Donovan hoped the future held happiness like that for him, as well.

Donovan turned his attention back to Joni, who was

explaining the way the weekend would work. Jericho would provide horses to everyone to ride to the campsite. The Double J had one of the best reputations in the region for training horses so Donovan knew the animals would be prime. From the looks of things, Jericho had improved on the stellar reputation his parents had earned.

Joni briefly explained the games and family competitions that would occur over the weekend. When she finished talking, Jericho took over and began directing people to their assigned horses. The tents and bags would be transported to the campsite by truck and would be waiting when the families arrived.

Donovan, Elias and Raven mounted their horses and Donovan led the way to the campsite. In addition to the map, there were markers pointing the way. Not that he needed directions. He knew this ranch like the back of his hand. As they rode, Donovan pointed to a tree. "That's where we built a treehouse. We turned it into a clubhouse."

"A clubhouse for boys," Raven pointed out. "Donovan had been my best friend until he decided I had cooties."

"Girl cooties," Donovan teased.

Elias laughed then turned to Jericho. "Who was in the club?"

"Me, Jericho and our friends Tony and Billy."

"What did you guys do?"

Donovan winked at Elias. "Secret boy stuff. I can't tell you in front of your mom, but I'll tell you later."

Elias nodded, satisfied. Donovan hoped that this pleasant conversation was the beginning of a breakthrough with his son. Of course, when Elias learned they hadn't done anything special in the club, that might change. Maybe he could convince Elias that they could start their own club. This time he'd definitely let Raven be a member.

Chapter Fifteen

Raven squeezed her hands together as she watched Donovan and Elias attempt to put up the tent. Her two men were sitting on the ground trying to figure out which pole went into which part of the fabric. They'd been at it for about twenty minutes. If she'd been in charge, the tent would have been up by now and they'd be rolling out their sleeping bags. But they'd thought they'd be able to do it better. Elias pulled on a pole and nearly whacked Donovan on the side of the head. Raven swallowed a giggle as well as her advice.

As they worked, Donovan regaled Elias with tales of his youth and his obviously embellished adventures with his friends. Elias was impressed, but Raven, not so much. After all, she'd been there. She remembered how much better she'd been at riding and swimming and fishing than he'd been. Heck, she'd been better at those things than all of the boys, which was no doubt the reason they'd excluded her from their club. She'd showed them up and their poor, male egos hadn't been able to handle it.

She hadn't been concerned about their egos then and she really wasn't concerned about them now. The only reason she wasn't jumping in and putting the tent up herself was that she wanted Elias and Donovan to continue to bond. Donovan deserved every opportunity to build a relationship with his son, and Elias deserved that chance, too, so she sat back and watched the comedy.

Looking around, she realized that Donovan and Elias weren't the only ones struggling to get their tent together. From what she could see, most of the other tents were in a similar state. Maybe ranchers spent so much time outside that they didn't camp for recreation. She loved sleeping under the stars, but maybe she was an aberration. Not that the ranchers were the only ones struggling. Dr. Tyler, Mayor Devlin and several other Sweet Briar residents didn't seem to be faring much better.

She heard laughter and turned back to her men. While she'd been looking around, they'd managed to get the poles through the frame and were now raising the tent. When it was finally standing, she applauded softly.

"Finished," Elias said proudly, wiping sweat from his brow.

"Not quite," she pointed out when Donovan nodded in agreement. "You need to nail in the tent pegs and set up the rain-fly."

"It's not going to rain," Elias said as if he were in charge of the weather.

"Better safe than sorry," Raven said. Hearing her words, she wondered if that had become her motto for life. After giving her heart to Donovan and having it smashed when he vanished, she'd become leery. That was most of the reason why she'd agreed to marry Carson. She didn't love him so her heart was safe. He could never hurt her.

She looked at her son hammering away at the tent pegs and wondered if she'd taught Elias to behave the same way. Was that why he'd been so willing to shove Donovan out of his life? Was he worried that Donovan would hurt him, leaving him brokenhearted? She didn't want her son to play it safe in life. Not with his emotions. She wanted him to experience the full joy of love even if it meant he might get hurt occasionally.

"Now we're finished," Elias said, dropping onto the grass beside her.

"My hero," Raven said then kissed his cheek.

"He had help," Donovan said. He sat beside her and pointed to his cheek.

Her stomach lurched and every nerve ending in her body was suddenly on high alert. Deciding to keep it light, she leaned over and gave him a peck. The stubble from his jaw tickled her lips and she felt woozy. Tiny stars danced on her skin, leaving bits of heat and light behind.

"Are we going to put our stuff in?" Elias said. "The games are going to start soon."

"Right." Donovan stood and held out his hand to help Raven stand. She took it and the warmth from his skin reached inside her chest and warmed her heart, and she smiled. She'd arranged this weekend so Donovan and Elias could rebuild their relationship, but there was no rule saying she couldn't use the time to see if anything remained of hers and Donovan's. And if there was? Well she was finished playing it safe. If there was something there, she was grabbing on to it with both hands.

Raven picked up her gear and stepped inside the tent. It wasn't huge, but it had enough space for two adults and a child. They selected their spots and unrolled their sleeping bags. She couldn't be sure, but it seemed as if Donovan had maneuvered it so that he would be sleeping next to her. Since she'd been plotting a way to do the same, he wouldn't get a complaint from her.

A bell rang and Elias raced outside. She and Donovan followed more slowly. When everyone was assembled, Joni began to speak. The first game was a scavenger hunt. Each family would be its own team. The numbers wouldn't be even because some families were larger than others and some of the kids were really little, but she reminded everyone this was all in good fun. There wouldn't be prizes. She hoped the end result would be closer family bonds. That should be reward enough.

"Now, each family should choose a representative to pick up your sealed envelope. It has a list of what you'll need to find. That person will be your team leader."

"Please pick me," Elias said.

Donovan and Raven exchanged looks and nodded.

"Thanks. I'll do a really good job." Elias raced to Joni's side. Raven noticed that most of the leaders were kids about Elias's age.

"This was a great idea," Donovan said.

"I wish I could take credit. This was Joni's brainchild. All I did was sign up."

"We have ten minutes to read the list and come up with a strategy," Elias said, running back over. "Miss Joni's going to blow a whistle letting us know when the game starts."

They sat and scanned the paper. There were thirty items on the list. Some of them could be found among the things they'd brought with them, like a comb or toothbrush. Others were things they would have to pick up in the surrounding area. Raven's competitive juices began to flow. Even though this was all in good fun, there was no reason not to try to win.

"Here's what I think we should do," she said, leaning in.

Donovan poked her in her side and she glared at him. He frowned and angled his head in Elias's direction. "We elected Elias to be our leader. He should come up with the plan. Go ahead, Elias."

"Well, Mom is better at this than I am. Maybe she should be the leader." Elias held out the list to her.

"No. Donovan is right. We chose you because we trust that you'll do a good job. Look how good you guys did with the tent." She hoped a strong wind didn't blow it over before she could sneak over and tighten it when they weren't looking. She might not care about the fragile male ego in general, but she did care specifically about Elias's ego.

Elias smiled again. "Here's my plan. I think we should find the stuff farthest away from camp first. Everybody will be looking for the same thing. We have to get them just in case they run out. Plus we won't be bumping into them. Then we can grab the stuff from our tent."

"Sounds good," Donovan said.

"Should we separate?" Raven asked. "We could get more things if we each took part of the list."

"We can't. Miss Joni said we all have to go together because it's a 'family' game."

Raven noticed that though he put emphasis on the word *family*, he didn't seem to have a problem thinking of Donovan as part of theirs. But she didn't think their issues had been resolved. She knew better. Still, this time of camaraderie was nice.

"Ten, nine, eight, seven, six…" Someone was counting down and kids began to join in, Elias included. "…five, four, three, two, one."

A whistle blew and there was a loud cheer before people began running pell-mell around the campground, looking for items on the list.

"This way," Donovan said when she and Elias would have followed the crowd. "There are a whole lot of wildflowers about a quarter mile from here."

"How do you know?" Elias asked, running behind Donovan.

"I told you. I used to hang out with Jericho when I was your age. We went all over the ranch just about every day."

A few minutes later they'd found a bunch of pretty flowers. It was almost a shame to pick them, but this was part of the game. "Where to next?"

Donovan shrugged. "What should we look for next, Elias?"

"The deer and the rabbit."

Raven held up her hand. "Just so you know, I'm not trying to catch either one of those. I believe they should be free in the wild."

"We only need pictures, Mom. Geez."

"There's a spring over that hill," Donovan said, pointing behind her shoulder. "If we're lucky and quiet, we just might spot some."

Elias grinned and they sprinted in the direction had

Donovan indicated. Donovan might not be able to pitch a tent to save his life, but he had a great memory and an excellent sense of direction. They found the spring in the meadow he'd indicated. They waited ten minutes before they spotted a deer. Elias snapped a picture with Donovan's phone. They waited a couple more minutes before giving up on the rabbit.

They found a few other items on the list and headed back to camp. There was a time limit on the game and they wanted to grab the things from their bags. They raced into the tent and Raven grabbed her bag. "I've got the comb."

Elias dumped out his backpack and held it up. "This is something gray."

Laughing, they pulled out other items and added them to the pile.

"One minute left." Joni's voice blasted into the tent. She'd somehow gotten her hands on a portable microphone.

Scooping up everything, they raced out of the tent to the finish line. Other families ran out, as well, carrying their treasures. When Joni announced there were ten seconds left, everyone joined in the countdown again. One little girl toddled over with her item just as the whistle blew.

Joni and several teenage volunteers counted the items each group had collected. Raven felt good about what they'd gathered. Although they hadn't found every item, twenty-four out of thirty wasn't bad.

While the judges were tallying the scores, Elias joined a group of boys his age who were standing on the edge of the crowd. She recognized most of them.

They were laughing raucously, no doubt recounting the fun they'd had on the scavenger hunt.

Raven looked at Donovan. "Elias often asks to go to the youth center, but I've told him no more often than not. It's so far away, you know? But now I'm wondering if that was a mistake. Listening to you talk about your friendship with Jericho, Tony and Billy, made me see what he's missing. There are no boys his age on the ranches nearby. His good friends live in town. He sees them all the time during the school year, but school is out now and it takes more of an effort to get them together. Unfortunately he doesn't get to hang out with them as much in the summer."

"Do you think he would enjoy going to the center? If so, I can drive him there sometimes. We could take turns. Or you could have his friends come out to the ranch some, too. Again I'm willing to help."

Raven nodded. It felt good not to have to do everything on her own.

"Okay, everyone. We're ready to announce the results," Joni said. "First, let me say you're all winners. No family found all of the items, but two families found twenty-six—the Tylers and the McDermotts. There was one item that only one family found, and that was the picture of the deer, found by the Reynolds-Cordero family. Congratulations to them and to all of you. You have a couple hours on your own. Dinner will be at five thirty. Until then, enjoy yourselves."

Elias raced back over. "Hey, there's a lake not too far from here. Me and my friends are going to go fishing. Is that okay, Mom?"

Raven started to say no but changed her mind. True, this was supposed to be a family weekend, but that didn't mean the three of them needed to spend every waking moment together. She glanced at Donovan, who shrugged. "Sure. But be careful."

"We will. Kenny's and Bobby's dads are coming, too. Bobby's dad is a doctor, so you don't have to worry about me getting sick." He darted into the tent and came back with his fishing pole.

"I'm sorry," she whispered to Donovan. It was clear that being excluded from the trip with the other fathers hurt his feelings.

"Don't worry about it. I haven't been around for most of his life so there's no reason for him to think of me as his dad."

"No reason other than the fact that you are."

Elias joined his friends and their fathers and they set off to the lake.

"How about a walk?" Donovan asked. He held out his hand and she took it. They had a couple of hours to kill so they might as well make the most of it. They went in the opposite direction from Elias so it wouldn't look like they were following him. They didn't speak until the sound of the camp no longer intruded on them.

"I never knew how beautiful the Double J was." Raven hadn't spent much time there before today. "It's almost as scenic as my parents' ranch."

"It is. If Jericho wasn't my oldest friend I'd be jealous."

"Your ranch has its own appeal."

"I missed it."

They came to a fallen log in an isolated part of the ranch and sat. They'd been holding hands the entire time they'd been walking and continued to do so. They stared into the horizon for a while. The companionable mood gradually shifted to a sexually charged one.

Suddenly Raven became more aware of the warmth of Donovan's hand, the rough calluses on his palm. His masculine scent surrounded her, tempting her, and with each breath, her longing for him grew in strength.

Unable to resist any longer, Raven lifted her head and stared into Donovan's eyes. They were dark with desire. He hesitated briefly, as if debating his next move, then brushed his lips against hers. Her mouth tingled at the contact and she sighed. He smiled at her response and a moment later, he deepened the kiss, wrapping her in his arms. Desire swept through her in intense waves, knocking over her common-sense reasons why they couldn't do this. She leaned in closer, pressing her body against his. She murmured his name as years of need to be in his embrace again was finally satisfied.

He ran his fingers down her back and shivers raced up her spine. Her head spinning, she tried to get even closer to him. She needed to be closer.

Without breaking the kiss, he slid his arms under her knees and gently lowered her to the ground. She pressed her hand to his chest and felt his heart thudding in a rapid beat that matched hers. The years fell away as the past and present merged. Being with Donovan again felt so right, so natural. Though they were no longer nineteen and their bodies had changed, they still fit together perfectly. It was as if the past ten years hadn't happened.

But they had. And as much as she wished she could, Raven knew they couldn't take up where they'd left off. Too much had happened. Too much could still happen.

She eased back, reluctantly ending the kiss. She needed to keep her head.

Blowing out a breath, she sat up and watched as Donovan did the same. He was breathing hard and her eyes were drawn to his muscular chest as it rose and fell with each breath. Instead of sitting on the log again, they remained seated on the ground and leaned against it. She brushed a hand over her hair in an attempt to remove the twigs and give it some sort of order then straightened her clothes. While working, she tried to organize her thoughts. He pulled a leaf from her hair, then gently caressed her cheek. Unable to resist, she leaned into his hand and kissed his work-roughened palm.

He dropped a kiss on her hair and her heart stuttered. Her eyes drifted shut and she basked in his nearness. Nothing could ever feel better than being close to Donovan. Yet she knew she needed to be strong. Sighing, she opened her eyes and met his gaze. The longing that remained nearly weakened her resolve. "What are we doing, Donovan?"

"I don't know." He flashed her a dimpled grin. "Making out?"

She laughed and swatted his arm, then leaned her head against his shoulder, unable to end all physical contact. "Besides that. Not that I didn't enjoy it, but we can't get caught up like this again. Everything is too complicated right now."

His lips turned down and his humor fled. He nodded. "I know. Hopefully we're getting to know each other again. Becoming friends. And if we're lucky, we might become more than that again."

"Do you think it can work? We're different people now."

He shook his head. "I thought that at first, too. I was wrong. We're the same people we were back then. We've just lived life apart for ten years. Our experiences helped us grow and mature. But still, underneath it all, we're still Raven and Donovan. Now we just need to find out if we mesh as well today as we did years ago."

One thing was certain, the physical attraction was just as strong now as it had been ten years ago. Even though she knew they needed clear minds to work though the situation, and that they didn't need the complication of a physical relationship making thinking more difficult, Raven kissed Donovan again. She kept it brief, believing she'd be able to control her desire, but she was wrong. She was ready to combust.

Donovan ran his finger over her cheek once more, then, expelling a long breath, stood and offered his hand and helped her to her feet. They didn't speak much as they walked back to camp, each pondering their own thoughts.

Donovan's words stuck with Raven the rest of the day and into the night. Dinner was a loud and fun affair, with families eating barbecued ribs, hot dogs, baked beans, potato salad and cake and ice cream at long tables. Elias seemed to know most of the kids, so she took the opportunity to get to know their parents.

After dinner they sat around a campfire and sung silly songs as well as traditional camping songs. Eventually the youngest kids began to fall asleep and their parents carried them to their tents. Even Elias started to droop. After the last song, they wandered back to their tent.

"This was so great," Elias said, pulling his dirty

T-shirt over his head and dropping it onto his sleeping bag. "I can't wait to see what we do tomorrow."

"Neither can I." Donovan pulled off his shirt, as well, revealing his muscular torso and ripped abs. If possible, his body had become even sexier since the afternoon they'd gotten drenched. And it had definitely felt wonderful this afternoon. But they'd agreed not to act on their attraction until they sorted out things.

Donovan caught her staring and flexed his pecs and winked. Raven broke eye contact. Fighting her feelings was going to be harder if he didn't cooperate.

"I need you guys to step out while I change into my pajamas."

Donovan chuckled. "That's going to be a problem since one of us has already conked out."

Raven looked at Elias. He'd climbed into his sleeping bag and was already sleeping. "Okay. Then you."

"You looked at mine. You didn't hear me complain."

Raven laughed and then shooed him from the tent. When she'd changed into her pink cotton pajamas, she opened the rain flap and let him back in.

"Wow."

"Stop it." She'd considered packing pajamas with long pants, but knew she'd be more comfortable in short bottoms. And if they happened to show off her legs? Well, there was nothing wrong with that.

Donovan dimmed the light in their lantern and they got into their sleeping bags. It was too hot to zip them all the way so they left them open from the waist up. She turned on her side to face him and he did the same.

"I never thought I'd be here again," Donovan whispered.

"Where? On the Double J?" The darkness of the tent

made everything seem intimate and despite what she'd said earlier, she was suddenly afraid of losing control of her emotions. When they were together like this, all she could think of was how much she loved being with him.

"With you." He reached out and caressed her cheek. It was dark, but she could feel his eyes boring into hers. She trembled. "I missed you every day of my life."

"I missed you, too."

He slid his hand until he was cupping her head then brushed his lips across hers. The kiss didn't last more than a second, but she felt a shift in their relationship. It had gone from just trying to be friends to a promise that they would somehow make a relationship between them work. That was good because she was pretty sure she'd fallen in love with him again. She was aware of all his warts and imperfections and knew there would be bumps in the road, but she was ready to travel it side by side.

He lay on his back and put his arm around her waist and pulled her to him. She put her head on his chest and closed her eyes, feeling his heart beating beneath her ear. For once in a long, long while, all was truly right with her world.

"I knew it," Elias's angry voice woke her and she blinked. "I knew you were trying to kiss my mom that day."

"What?" She opened her eyes and sat up, trying to get her bearings.

"He was only pretending to be my friend because he wants you to be his girlfriend again."

"That's not true," Donovan said. "You're my son and I love you. Nothing and nobody means more to me than you. I'd do anything to be a part of your life."

Chapter Sixteen

"No you don't." Elias backed away, but Donovan was too quick and grabbed him by the arms before he could run from the tent.

"Listen, son."

"Don't call me that. I'm not your son."

"But you are. And you mean more to me than anyone else in the world."

"Then why did you leave?" Elias's voice wobbled and Donovan knew this was his best chance to reach his son.

"Because I had to." Donovan glanced at Raven, who was sitting on her sleeping bag. She looked pained. No doubt seeing Elias so upset hurt her heart. Donovan sat, then pulled Elias down beside him and edged closer to Raven.

"Why? Did somebody make you?" Elias's voice was filled with sarcasm.

"Yes."

"What?" Donovan's answer took the wind from Elias's sails. "Is that true, Mom? Did somebody make him leave me?"

Raven nodded.

"Then why didn't you tell me?" Elias's anger found a new target in his mother. "Why did we stay here? We should have gone with him."

"Whoa. Hold on. You've got it all wrong. I told you before, none of this is your mother's fault. She didn't know where I went. Or why I left."

"Why not?"

"Because I never got the chance to tell her."

Elias opened his mouth again, probably with the intent of asking why again, so Donovan stopped him. "Just listen, okay?"

"All right."

"I had been with your mom. I left her to go to Sweet Briar. Before I got to town, I saw a crime being committed. The criminal saw me. He knew who I was. He said if I didn't leave town right then and stay gone forever, he'd hurt me. And your mom. So I left and didn't come back. She didn't get a chance to tell me about you."

"If you had known about me, would you have stayed?"

Donovan heard the plea in his son's voice, the yearning to be told that he mattered to Donovan. "No."

Elias sagged and his eyes filled with tears at what he perceived as rejection.

"I would have loved you too much to risk your life. Knowing about you would have given me one more reason to leave. And one more reason to stay away."

Elias pondered that for a while. "You would have left because you loved me?"

"Yes. To keep you safe."

"I wish you had been here. I always wanted a dad."

"I wish I could have been here, too. But I'm here now. And I would like to be your dad."

Elias rubbed his forearm across his eyes. "For how long? What if you decide you don't want to be my dad anymore? What if you want to leave a second time?"

Donovan's eyes misted over and he blinked to clear them. "I'll always want to be your dad. Always. And I'll never want to leave you."

"What if that bad man tries to make you leave again?"

"That won't happen."

"How do you know?"

"Because he died. He can never hurt our family again."

Elias nodded. "Okay."

Donovan pulled Elias into a tight hug. "I love you, son."

"I love you, too, Dad."

Donovan closed his eyes and inhaled deeply. For the first time in ten years he felt as if everything in his life was right again. He glanced over at Raven. Tears shimmered in her eyes. No, everything in his life wasn't right again. Although he and Raven were getting close again, they hadn't verbally committed to each other. Still he believed she was the only one who could fill the hole in his heart. He opened his arms and she joined in the embrace. Now he knew what it would take to truly be happy. He needed his family. He wanted his son, true, but more than that, he wanted Raven back in his life. He wanted to marry her the way he'd planned to years ago. He believed she felt the same but he wasn't one hundred percent sure. But if there was even the slightest bit of love in her heart, he intended to help it grow.

* * *

"I wish we could stay longer, don't you, Daddy?"

"Yep. Maybe we can go camping again this summer. What do you think, Raven?"

"Sure." What could she say? That being around him was making her imagination do crazy things? The day had been filled with fun games for the entire family. The three-legged relay races had been the worst. Having her leg tied to Donovan's and inhaling his masculine scent had been her own private torture. Being so close to him had made her weak in the knees and she'd barely made it from the start line to the finish line. For once her competitive nature had taken a back seat to her desire.

The events had been designed to bring families closer together emotionally, and they'd been successful. She felt closer to Donovan than she ever had. And it was good to see Elias and Donovan bonding, too. But all of that emotional closeness had been accomplished by physical closeness. Donovan didn't appear affected by all of the touching and hand-holding they'd had to do. He hadn't mentioned the kiss. It was as if they hadn't shared those quiet moments.

Raven rolled up her sleeping bag, shoved it into its fabric carrying sack and pulled the string to tighten it. She struggled to get her doubts under control. After all, there hadn't been time for private conversations.

Was he supposed to talk about his feelings during the frozen T-shirt race or glow-in-the-dark bowling? With activities planned for just about every waking hour, conversation had been limited. And once Elias had decided Donovan was his favorite person on the planet, he'd stuck to him like glue. He'd moved his sleeping bag closer to Donovan's, making talking impossible, not that Donovan appeared interested. He was floating on the high of having his son acknowledge him and welcome him into his life.

And Elias? He was in hog heaven. More than once he'd said how great it was to have a mom and a dad just like his friends. He was definitely Team Donovan. This weekend had lived up to its promise. Elias and Donovan were even closer than Raven had hoped.

Maybe this weekend had worked too well because there was no doubt that she'd fallen in love with Donovan again.

"Don't you think this was the best, Mom?" Apparently he'd heard the ambivalence in her voice, which was amazing given the fact that he'd been focused on his father.

"Yep. I can't think of the last time I had this much fun." And the truth was she couldn't remember laughing as hard as she had while playing those wacky games.

"Hey. Dad, do you want to come over for dinner tonight?"

Raven smiled despite the turmoil his question caused inside her. Elias seemed to be unable to decide between calling Donovan *Dad* or *Daddy* and was trying them out to see which one fit best. He'd tried *Father* on for size but had wrinkled his nose, easily discarding that title. Raven held her breath while she waited for Donovan's answer.

"I'd love to."

"Great. Mom is the best cook in the world."

"Your mom is the best at a lot of things."

Raven felt her cheeks heat. "Okay. Enough flattery,

guys. My parents have plans tonight so I'm already committed to cooking."

"You don't have to cook," Donovan said. "Let me take you guys to the diner."

"Yeah!" Elias readily agreed. "They have the best burgers. And I love their shakes. They always put a cherry on top. If you ask, they'll let you have two."

"I guess that settles it." She really hadn't felt like cooking anyway. But she hadn't expected to have dinner with Donovan. After spending the entire weekend together, she was overdosing on his nearness.

"Okay. Let's get going. I'll drop you guys off and pick you up in an hour or so."

Instead of riding horses back to the house, the campers were driven back in trucks. When they reached Camille and Jericho's house, they thanked the couple and then got into Donovan's truck. The ride home was a lot less tense than it had been coming here.

Elias jumped out of the truck and hustled around to the back to help Donovan unload their gear. Elias grabbed his backpack and sleeping bag then headed for the house singing one of the silly songs they'd learned. Raven reached for her equipment but Donovan grabbed it. "I have it."

"Thanks."

They climbed the stairs in silence. He was so close, the heat from his body knocked into her, making her shiver. She'd always found Donovan attractive and time and distance hadn't changed that. If anything, he was sexier than he'd ever been. And the anger, tension and mistrust between them was gone, no longer keeping her from fully appreciating what was right in front of her eyes.

He dropped her bags inside the door then leaned against the wall. "I'm really looking forward to dinner tonight."

"Me, too."

He brushed his lips across her cheek and then left.

Raven stood there for a moment then looked up. Elias was staring at her.

"Is Dad gone?"

"Yes."

"Okay. Then why are you standing there looking all goofy?"

She shook her head. "Who are you calling goofy, young man?"

Elias laughed and took off running. "Just you, Mom. You're the goofiest of all goofs."

Raven laughed as she chased him up the stairs and headed to her bathroom to take a quick shower and get dressed for dinner. Twenty minutes later she was standing in her room, debating over what to wear. The diner was casual eating, but she'd spent the weekend in shorts and T-shirts. Although that or jeans were her usual uniform—she lived on a ranch for goodness' sake—she didn't want to wear them tonight. But she didn't want to look ridiculous in something too dressy. That would look like she was trying too hard. In the end she settled on a floral sundress and sandals. She braided her hair into one long French braid down her back and fastened a rubber band on the end to keep it from coming loose. She added simple stud earrings and the bracelet Donovan had given her for her birthday and then went downstairs to wait.

"Wow," Elias said. "You look really pretty, Mom.

Are you trying to make Daddy want to be your boy-friend?"

Raven nearly choked. Did it look like she was trying to get Donovan's attention? If a nine-year-old thought so, then she might be sending that message. Maybe she should change. She certainly didn't want Donovan to think she was laying some sort of trap. She'd told her-self to go for it, but that was before her doubts began to sprout and take root. She was spinning around to head back upstairs when the doorbell rang. Elias had the door open before she was out of the room.

"It's Dad," Elias said unnecessarily as they stepped into the room.

"Wow," Donovan said. Appreciation and desire shone in his eyes. "You're beautiful."

"You don't look too shabby yourself." He was wear-ing khakis and a gray polo that matched his eyes. So he'd dressed up a little, too. She relaxed and decided to stop overthinking things.

"Hey, Dad," Elias said, oblivious to the sexual un-dercurrents between his parents. "Do you think I could borrow some of your comics? I'm sorry I was so mean to you before. I won't act that way again."

"Of course. If it's not too late, we can stop by after dinner and you can get them."

"Do you think we could get them now? That way we don't have to worry about it being too late."

"Sure. That should be okay."

"Thanks, Dad."

As they walked down the stairs to the truck, Dono-van pulled Raven aside. "Did I just make a mistake?

Should I have told him no or given him some sort of lecture?"

"I don't think so. Elias is usually a good kid. That was a pretty extraordinary situation, so I think it was okay to let him borrow the books again."

Donovan smiled. "That's a relief. I don't want to mess up this dad thing."

"You'll make mistakes. Everybody does, myself included. All you can do is your best. As long as you're acting out of love and considering what's best for him, you'll be fine."

Apparently having dinner at the diner was a popular idea for many of the families who'd attended the camping weekend at the Double J Ranch. Elias waved to several of his friends. When he saw Kenny, he raced to join him and his brother at their table. Elias had brought one of the comic books inside with him and showed it to them. They scooted over in their booth and Elias sat. Three heads immediately bent over the book.

"Hi," Raven said to Kenny's parents. "We didn't mean to intrude."

"On our family time?" Kenny's mother laughed. "Don't worry about it. We did plenty of bonding over the weekend. If you want, Elias can eat with us. Unless you were planning a family dinner."

Raven glanced at Donovan, who shrugged. "Nah. We're good."

"Then let him stay. I'll put the book in my purse when the food comes."

"I'd appreciate it," Donovan said. He put his hand on Raven's waist and led her to their table. The warmth from his touch sent tingles shimmying down her spine.

When they were seated, she looked up into his eyes. The look he gave her was intense. He covered her hand with his. "Would it be wrong of me to say that I'm glad our son is eating dinner with his friends?"

Raven laughed. "Don't tell me fatherhood is losing its luster already?"

"Never. There's just something to be said about having dinner alone with a beautiful woman."

Her heart skipped a beat. "You don't have to use your considerable charm on me. I'm not going to try to keep you from him."

"The thought never crossed my mind."

"So what's with the compliments?"

"They're sincerely made. You've always been gorgeous. You know that. And if your former fiancé didn't tell you that, then he must have been blind."

Raven didn't know what to say in response to that, but, she knew she didn't want to talk about Carson. "Okay. Thanks for the compliment."

"So now that you're a free woman, I need to know, is your heart open to love again?"

She trembled. Talk about going from zero to one hundred in under a second. "Why?"

"Because I missed you like crazy. I feel like our relationship was interrupted. I can't sit here and say that we would still be together now if not for Karl Rivers, but we might. I feel like there's still something between us. I don't know how much of it is the memory of what we had, and how much of it is new and if any of it is real."

"You just put it out there, don't you?"

"I've lost so much time. I don't want to waste more playing games. Do you?"

She shook her head. "No. I wasted enough time. I don't want to waste more."

He smiled and gave her hand a gentle squeeze before pulling his hand away. "So does this mean you're my girl again?"

"Are you asking me to go steady?"

"I guess I am."

"Then I'm saying yes."

They talked and laughed over dinner, but as he pulled in front of her house, she couldn't remember what they'd talked about. All she could recall was how he'd made her feel. And that had been cherished. Valued. Loved. It might be too soon to think about becoming a family, but she couldn't help herself. She'd yearned for Donovan for ten long years. And now they might actually get the happily-ever-after she'd dreamed of.

Elias got out of the truck and stumbled up the stairs. It had taken all of his energy to stay awake on the ride home and Raven could tell he would be asleep as soon as his head hit the pillow.

"Bye, Daddy. See you tomorrow."

"See you, son."

Raven's parents were home now and they were sitting on the front porch. When Raven and Donovan reached them, her father nudged her mother and then stood. Marilyn frowned at him and stood slowly.

"Did you have a good time this weekend?" Rudy asked.

"The best."

"Glad to hear it. We'll help Elias get ready for bed. You young people sit down and enjoy this beautiful night." He gave Donovan's shoulder an affectionate squeeze as he passed by. "Good to have you home. I hope to see more of you."

"Thanks. It's great to be home."

Raven noticed her mother went inside without speaking. Clearly, Marilyn was not pleased that Donovan was going to be a part of their lives again. Raven just didn't understand it. Her mother had loved Donovan and had been heartbroken when she'd believed he was dead. She should be rejoicing that he was alive and well. If not for Raven and Elias's sakes, then for Lena Cordero's. Donovan's mother had been Marilyn's best friend. There was no understanding her mother and Raven was going to stop trying. Once Marilyn saw Donovan's sincerity, she would come around.

When Donovan took her hand and led her to the love seat, all thought of her mother vanished. They sat and he draped his arm over the back of the sofa, letting his hand dangle over her shoulder. She leaned her head into his elbow and closed her eyes. This was what real happiness felt like. Like flying and falling and dancing while listening to the most beautiful sounds ever created. If only she could stay like this forever.

Donovan inhaled and Raven's delicate scent tantalized his senses. It had taken a bit of effort, but they'd finally resolved all of their issues and, after what seemed like forever, he had her in his arms again. She felt just as good as he remembered, better than in his dreams. As they sat there, his longing for her grew and he pulled her into his arms. Their gazes met and held. When he saw his desire reflected in her eyes, he leaned over and kissed her.

Her lips were so soft, her taste so sweet. She moaned softly against his lips and he deepened the kiss. All the years of loneliness melted away and the hole in his soul closed. He could have kissed her for hours but instead he eased away. He had a feeling Marilyn was somewhere seething and could burst onto the porch at any moment. He needed to talk with her so they could resolve their problems. They'd gotten along in the past. He hoped that once she knew he loved Raven and Elias and would never leave them again, they'd get along like old times.

He leaned his forehead against Raven's. They were both breathing hard. "I should probably go. We both need to get up early."

"I know. But I don't want to say goodbye."

"Neither do I. That's a good thing."

"Only you would think that." She cupped his face in her hands and then gave him a kiss that left him gasping for breath and longing for more. She stood and put her hand on her hip then gave him a saucy wink. "Still think leaving is a good thing?"

He reached for her but she darted away. "Not good. But wise. I'll talk to you later."

When he arrived home, he was pleased to see that his parents hadn't waited up for him. They finally believed that he wasn't going to disappear again. When he reached his room, he got undressed, climbed into bed and grabbed his cell phone.

Raven answered on the first ring. "I was wondering if you would call."

"Really?"

"No."

He leaned his pillow against the headboard and sat up. He had to get up early, but he wasn't ready to let the night end. Instead he listened to Raven's voice and imagined the life they were going to have together.

Chapter Seventeen

"You're making a mistake."

Same song, different verse. Raven slid the bracelet over her wrist before turning to face her mother. Raven had hoped they'd resolved this issue the last time they'd talked about Donovan, but that had been based on wishful thinking. "Then it's my mistake to make."

Her mother frowned. "Not alone. You're not the only one with something to lose."

"Elias is happy to have his father around. You know that."

"I do. And he should be. I just wonder about this sudden romance between you and Donovan."

"We dated for years. I wouldn't call our relationship sudden. Our son is nine years old."

"Yes. And it seems to me that Donovan's attention has more to do with Elias than it does with you."

"You're wrong." Raven infused her voice with confidence even though her doubt surfaced again. He had said he'd do anything to have Elias in his life. Surely he hadn't meant pretending to be in love with her. After all, she'd already told him she wouldn't stand in the way of his relationship with their son. He could see Elias any time he wanted.

"Am I? Tell me, was Donovan interested in getting back with you before or after he found out about Elias?"

Raven closed her eyes and wished she could close her ears as well. It had happened all at once. But still, she did remember what Donovan had said that first day. He'd told her he'd hoped they could still be friends. *Friends.* It wasn't until he'd seen Elias that he'd wanted more. "That doesn't prove anything."

"Then you know I'm right. For goodness sake, don't let that man hurt you again."

"Why are you so sure that Donovan doesn't want me? Do you think there's something about me that makes me unlovable?"

"I never said that."

"Then what? What is it that has you so set against our being together?"

"People don't change He broke your heart. Your spirit. He broke you. He'll do it again."

Raven was tempted to tell her mother the real reason Donovan had left. Carson had taken his mother to stay with her sister and then left town himself. He'd called a couple of days ago to let her know he'd identified the man his father had killed. Carson is currently in Tennessee, trying to track down the man's family so he wouldn't know she'd revealed anything. But she'd know. She'd given her word and intended to keep it. Besides, she wanted her mother to see the man Donovan was now. And she needed to convince her mother that Donovan wanted her and not just Elias. "Mom, I'm not nineteen and pregnant. I'm not confused and trying to figure out what happened to the man I love. Whether or not things work between us, I'm going to be fine. And I'll make sure that Elias is fine. Donovan will, too."

"I just don't trust him."

"Just give him a chance. Please. He's a good man."

"You sound just like your father."

"When has Dad ever been wrong?"

"Not often. And don't you tell him I said that, either."

"It'll be our secret."

"I just want you to be careful. Guard your heart if only for a little while. You've gotten swept away again. Take your time before you fall in love." With those final words, Raven's mother gave her a kiss on the cheek and walked away.

"But I'm already in love," Raven murmured to herself. She'd tried holding back, keeping a firm handle on her emotions, but it had proved impossible. Over the past few weeks Donovan had managed to loosen the grip she'd held on her feelings. He'd charmed her and wooed her. He'd just been so kind. So open and honest. They'd spent time together with Elias as a family—they'd taken him to see that superhero movie he'd been dying to see—and they'd spent time together as a couple.

As much as she loved their time together, she always looked forward to the end of the night when Donovan would hold her in his arms and kiss her good-night. Each kiss had grown more passionate and she was all but ready to combust when he released her. Once she regained control of herself, she would rush into her room, grab her phone and wait for him to call. They'd not only resumed their practice of talking every night, they now spoke every morning. She smiled as she recalled the delight in his voice when she'd called him the morning after their camping trip, so she'd begun waking him up each morning to talk before they started their day.

The only problem was he never told her that he loved her. Her stomach churned with unease as she considered the possibility that she might be the only one in love. She told herself it was only her insecurity talking, but the feeling didn't go away. But then she hadn't told him that she loved him, either. It could be that he was just as unsure as she was.

Except, Donovan had been direct about everything so far. He'd come out and told her what he'd wanted. He wanted to see if the love was still there. Perhaps for him it hadn't been. If he loved her, he would say so. The fact that he hadn't could only mean one thing. He hadn't fallen back in love with her.

She shook her head, refusing to let the negative thoughts take hold. She wouldn't even be entertaining these ideas if her mother hadn't planted the seeds of doubt.

Taking one last look in the mirror, she straightened her blouse and then dashed downstairs. Elias was lying on the floor, a box filled with comics beside him. He'd been thrilled to discover that Donovan had every comic in several series and was willing to let him borrow them, a box at a time, so he could read them in chronological order.

She nudged him with her toe. "What time is Kenny's mom getting here?"

He glanced at the clock on his phone. "In thirty-seven minutes."

"Then don't you think you should get ready? It's not polite to keep someone waiting."

Elias closed the comic, slid it into the plastic sleeve, then found the correct place in the box and put it inside. Raven was happy to see that he was taking good care of Donovan's treasured collection.

"Is that why you're always ready way before Dad gets here." It had taken a while, but Elias had settled on Dad as the name for Donovan. Elias looked up at her and his eyes grew wide. "Wow. You look really pretty."

"Thanks."

"Wouldn't it be great if you and Dad got married? Then we could all live together in the same house. And I would be able to read his comics anytime I want. He's going to build a house, you know."

"He told you that?"

"Yeah. Didn't he tell you?"

Once. A long time ago when they'd been young dreamers. They'd even gone riding one day and found the perfect spot. It was close enough to his parents' house to be neighbors, but far enough away for everyone to have privacy.

"When did he tell you?"

Elias shrugged. "I don't know. One time when we went fishing. We didn't catch anything, but it was fun talking."

"Did he say anything else?" Raven asked.

"I told him I wished we all lived in the same house so he said he would work on it. He said he wanted to live with me, too. He misses me, you know. He said living together would make everything perfect. I think that means he's going to ask you to marry him so he can live with me all the time. If he does, all you have to do is say yes. Then I get to have a mom and dad all the time just like Kenny."

Raven's heart, which had been wobbling, tumbled to her toes. Maybe there was a reason he hadn't told her that he loved her. He didn't and he didn't want to lie to her. He wanted his son. Donovan would never wrench Elias away from her, so instead he was working on a plan that would let them share their son. They'd both get the joy of seeing Elias every day and watching him grow up. All of the dinners and dancing had been part of his scheme to woo her. He'd been talking about how well they fit together, as if they had never been apart. He wasn't trying to win her back. He was trying to win her over.

She pushed those thoughts away. She was jumping to conclusions. After all, she wanted to live with Donovan, too. Maybe after their rough start he wanted to make sure Elias was on board before he proposed to Raven. That made sense, didn't it? Or was she trying too hard to justify his behavior? Darn her stupid doubts.

Elias jumped up. "I'm going to get ready before Kenny's mom gets here. I hope you and Dad have fun. And remember, if he asks you to marry him, say yes."

Raven watched her son race from the room. If only it was so easy. Of course it would have been if not for the doubts that had taken root. She needed to know that Donovan really loved her. That shouldn't be too hard to discover, should it? But until she knew for sure, she needed to protect her heart. She couldn't allow herself to fall more deeply in love with him until she knew he returned her feelings.

* * *

"Mom's not coming with us," Elias said. He'd charged out of the house before Donovan had gotten the key out of the ignition. He was glad to spend time with his son, but he'd been looking forward to seeing Raven.

"Is she sick?"

"Nope. She just said she had something that she needed to do. I think she knows she's not going to win. She doesn't bowl as good as we do."

That couldn't be it. Raven was competitive but she didn't care about losing at bowling. She thought the whole game was ridiculous and only played at all because it turned out that Elias was a natural and she wanted to encourage him. Besides, Donovan knew she was throwing their games so Elias could win.

Ordinarily he wouldn't worry, but this was the third date she'd backed out of in a week. The other two times she'd given the flimsiest excuses. And though he called her every night, she seemed distant and ended the calls after only a few minutes. And she'd stopped calling him in the morning. When he'd asked her why, she said she'd overslept. He didn't believe it for a minute, but he'd had no way of proving otherwise.

Something was wrong. He replayed their last real conversation but didn't recall anything that would explain why Raven had suddenly become distant. If he didn't know better, he'd think she was trying to cool things between them and eventually end their relationship.

But he did know better. Raven loved him. Just as he loved her. So how had things gotten derailed?

"Aren't we going?" Elias asked.

Donovan nodded. He didn't want to start breaking promises to Elias. Their relationship was too new and too fragile. So although Donovan wanted to talk to Raven and find out what he'd done wrong, it would have to wait.

As they drove, Elias chattered about the activities he'd been participating in at the youth center. Raven and Donovan had agreed that it was good for Elias to spend time with kids his age, so they made sure he went to the center a couple of times a week. Donovan's attention was split between his thoughts and Elias's conversation, so it took a minute for his son's words to penetrate his mind.

"What did you just say?"

Elias gave him an odd look. "I said I told mom that you want us all to live together. You know, to make up for not getting to live with me when I was a kid. I told her that when you ask her to marry you she should say yes."

"What did she say??"

"Nothing."

"Are you sure?"

"Yep. She'll probably say yes. Then we can be a real family."

"Aren't you the matchmaker."

"You said you'd do anything to have me in your life. That means you'd marry mom, right?"

"Please tell me you didn't say that to your mom."

"I only reminded her. After all, she was there when you said it."

Donovan groaned. "When did you say this?"

Elias's brow wrinkled as he thought. Then his eyes lit up as he remembered. "When I spent the night with Kenny."

That was right when Raven had begun to pull away. She'd been quiet that night, pleading headache so that they could end the date early. Surely she hadn't believed Elias. She had to know that he loved her. After all he was doing everything in his power to show Raven how he felt. Everything except the most important thing. He hadn't told her that he loved her. And he did. He loved her with his whole heart. He thought his actions would speak louder than his words and remove any doubts she had about how he felt for her. In this case, words would have been better. He was going to set the record straight as soon as possible.

"Hey, Elias, would it be okay with you if we didn't go bowling now?"

"Oh, man. Why?"

"There's something we need to do."

"You mean you aren't taking me home so you can do something more fun or important?"

"No. There's nothing more fun than being with you. And nobody is more important to me than you."

Elias grinned. "I know."

"Your mom is very important to me, too."

"I know. You love her."

"I do. But I'm not sure she knows that. Even though she knows why I left her before, she might still have doubts about my feelings now. So I'm going to need your help convincing her."

Elias nodded, clearly on board with the plan. Donovan hoped it wasn't too late.

"Mom."

Raven heard her name being called one minute before her son burst into the kitchen. She hadn't expected him to be back so soon. They'd only been gone a couple of hours. Usually he wasn't home from his outings with Donovan until bedtime. After placing the tray of cookies in the oven, she turned. "What?"

"You need to come with me." He grabbed her hand and start pulling her out the back door. He paused and then dashed across the room and turned off the oven. This must be important if he was willing to delay cookies.

"Where are we going?"

"I can't tell you. It's a surprise."

She stepped outside and froze. Evening Dream was saddled and waiting. Donovan was sitting on Zeus. When he saw her, he dismounted and held out a hand. Without thinking, she put her hand into his. "What's going on?"

"We're going for a ride."

"I'm busy."

She tried to pull away, but Donovan wouldn't let her go. "This won't take long."

"Just go, Mom. Please. It's important," Elias urged.

Telling herself that nothing could hurt her heart more than it already was, Raven allowed Donovan to help her onto her horse and waited until he was beside her. "This is your show."

A look of disappointment flashed on his face and she felt guilty. There was no reason for her to be snippy just because he didn't love her. She had a feeling he was going to propose to her. Why else would he be making such a big production of this? Why else would Elias be so excited? They both expected that she would say yes and that they would become one big happy family.

Unfortunately there was no way that was going to

happen. She loved Donovan. She loved Elias. But she was going to disappoint both of them when she said no. And she had to say no. She loved Donovan too much to say yes. Unrequited love would turn to resentment and anger and ruin any chance they had of remaining friends.

They traveled across her family's ranch and then headed across his. She thought he would take her to their special place, but he didn't go in that direction. Where was he going? Her heart sank as she thought he might go to the spot where they'd once considered building a house. That would be too cruel. But he didn't head there, either. She decided to stop trying to guess and just calm down. Thinking of all the possibilities was only stressing her out.

She turned her attention to her surroundings, hoping that focusing on nature would calm her spirit. The sky was a beautiful blue without a cloud in sight. The sun was shining but it wasn't too hot. This actually was a perfect day. Though she wasn't exactly relaxed, she was no longer tense.

After twenty more minutes, Donovan slowed and then stopped his horse, so she did the same. They dismounted. He led her to a tree.

"Where are we?"

"You don't recognize this place?"

She looked around and searched for something familiar. Nothing here triggered her memory. "No. Should I?"

He smiled. "No. We've never been here before."

"Then why did you ask me that?"

"I'm trying to make a point."

"Well, try again. I missed it."

"We've never been here before. It has no tie to our

past. This is where we can make a new beginning." He closed his eyes briefly. When he opened them, they were so clear she could see straight to his soul. "When I came back, I wanted so badly to make up for everything I'd lost in the past. I tried to pick up my life and make up for lost time. That's not possible. I know that now.

"Right here in this place, I want to begin the future. With you. The past is over. But the present is good. And the future looks wonderful. That is, if you'll share it with me."

"Donovan…"

"Shh."

He reached into his pocket and pulled out a small box then knelt. She knew what was coming and her heart began to flutter. Despite herself, she wanted to hear the words.

"I love you, Raven. Will you marry me?"

Her heart ached and tears flooded her eyes then overflowed, sliding down her cheeks. "I can't, Donovan."

"Of course you can."

"I know you want to have Elias in your life. I won't stand in the way. You don't have to marry me for that to happen."

"I know that. But I want more than Elias in my life. I want you."

"Donovan, stop."

"I know you think I don't love you, but I do." He pulled out a Swiss army knife and pricked his finger then held out his hand.

"What are you doing?"

"I didn't let you become a member of my club when we were kids. But starting now, I want us to be in the same club."

She shook her head. "This won't change anything."

"So then there's no reason not to do it."

Shaking her head, she took the knife and pricked her finger. Then he rubbed their fingers together. "You know that is so unsanitary."

"Don't ruin the moment."

He stepped up to the huge tree and carved their initials and then scratched a heart around them. "I love you, Raven."

Her heart cracked but she kept her voice steady. "I wish it was true."

"It is."

"Then I wish I could believe it."

"What's holding you back?"

"Fear. Doubt. I want to trust this feeling but how can I? You want to be a part of Elias's life. If that means marrying me, then I guess that's a sacrifice you're willing to make."

"So what you're saying is you need proof that I was interested before."

"Yes."

"I can't…" He stopped and then his eyes lit up. "Come on."

"What?"

He didn't answer but rather hopped onto his horse. More than a little curious and incredibly hopeful, she jumped on hers, as well. As they galloped across the ranch, she wondered how he could prove that his feelings were real and that he did love her. She hoped he could. And maybe she should believe him. After all, he was going through a lot of trouble if he only wanted Elias.

When they reached her ranch, he swung down from

his horse and once more she followed suit. After asking a ranch hand to care for the horses, he grabbed her by the hand and pulled her into the kitchen. Elias, her parents and his parents looked up.

"Did she say yes?" Elias asked.

"Not yet."

"Mom," Elias groaned. The adults muttered and looked puzzled. Even Marilyn seemed disappointed. What was that about?

"Give me a couple more minutes."

He led her through the house and onto the front porch. "Sit down."

"Okay." Her heart was pounding. She didn't understand what a change of scenery would do, but she was willing to go with it.

"I just hope they're still there."

"What?"

He opened the chest in front of the love seat. "Yes."

She leaned forward. "What?"

"Do you remember that night I came over for dinner the first time?"

She nodded. If she remembered correctly, he'd been acting strangely when she'd opened the door. It was as if he'd been running.

"At the time I was thinking about dating you, but it was too soon. And you were still so angry about me not telling you why I had stayed away. But I was interested then. And I wanted the chance to get back together again. And it had absolutely nothing to do with Elias. It was you. Only you. It's always been you."

"Okay."

He pulled out a bundle of dried flowers. Although no longer fresh, they were still beautiful. "I was going to give these to you at the time, but it seemed too…obvious. Too much too soon. I didn't think you were ready to accept anything from me, especially my love."

"Are you saying you loved me then?"

He breathed out. "Yes. I'm saying I loved you then. I've been trying to figure out if the love I feel is from the past or the present. It finally hit me that it's both. I loved you then. I love you now. I'll love you always."

"Oh."

He held out the ring again.

Throwing caution to the wind, she took it. "I've always loved you, too."

He pulled her into his arms and kissed her deeply. Her knees weakened and her heart filled with love. She was happier than she'd ever been in her life.

She heard cheering and turned around.

"Well?" Elias asked.

Donovan nodded. "She said yes."

Their families cheered and even her mother looked excited. Elias joined in the hug and a feeling of contentment like nothing she'd ever felt filled her. Finally she had everything she wanted. She was back with the man she loved. Her rancher had returned.

* * * * *

*Make sure to return to
Sweet Briar, North Carolina,
when Kathy Douglass's
Sweet Briar Sweethearts
series continues
in August 2019!*

Only from Harlequin Special Edition.

#2683 GUARDING HIS FORTUNE

The Fortunes of Texas: The Lost Fortunes • by Stella Bagwell

Savannah Fortune is off-limits, and bodyguard Chaz Mendoza knows it. The grad student he's been hired to look after is smart, opinionated—and rich. What would she want with a regular guy like Chaz? Her family has made it clear he has no permanent place in her world. But Chaz refuses to settle for anything less...

#2684 THE LAWMAN'S ROMANCE LESSON

Forever, Texas • by Marie Ferrarella

When Shania Stewart tells Deputy Daniel Tallchief that he needs to lighten up with his wild younger sister, the handsome lawman doesn't know whether to ignore her or kiss her. But Shania knows. It's going to take a carefully crafted lesson plan to tutor this cowboy in love.

#2685 TO KEEP HER BABY

The Wyoming Multiples • by Melissa Senate

After Ginger O'Leary learns she's pregnant, it's time for a whole new Ginger. James Gallagher is happy to help, but after years of raising his siblings, becoming attached isn't in the plan. But neither is the way his heart soars every time he and Ginger match wits. What will it take for these two opposites to realize that they're made for each other?

#2686 AN UNEXPECTED PARTNERSHIP

by Teresa Southwick

Leo Wallace had been duped—hard—once before, so he refuses to take Tess's word when she says she's pregnant. Now she wants Leo's help to save her family business, too. Leo agrees to be the partner Tess needs. But it's going to take a paternity test to make him believe this baby is his. He just can't trust his heart again...no matter what it's saying.

#2687 THE NANNY CLAUSE

Furever Yours • by Karen Rose Smith

When Daniel Sutton's daughters rescue an abandoned calico, the hardworking attorney doesn't expect to be sharing his home with a litter of newborns! And animal shelter volunteer Emma Alvarez is transforming the lives of Daniel and his three girls. The first-time nanny is a natural with kids and pets. Will that extend to a single father ready to trust in love again?

#2688 HIS BABY BARGAIN

Texas Legends: The McCabes • by Cathy Gillen Thacker

Ex-soldier turned rancher Matt McCabe wants to help his recently widowed friend and veterinarian, Sara Anderson. She wants him to join her in training service dogs for veterans—oddly, he volunteers to take care of her adorable eight-month-old son, Charley, instead. This "favor" feels more like family every day...though their troubled pasts threaten a happy future.

YOU CAN FIND MORE INFORMATION ON UPCOMING HARLEQUIN® TITLES, FREE EXCERPTS AND MORE AT WWW.HARLEQUIN.COM.

HSECNM0319

SPECIAL EXCERPT FROM

H HARLEQUIN®

SPECIAL EDITION

*When Shania Stewart tells Deputy Daniel Tallchief that
he needs to lighten up with his wild younger sister,
the handsome lawman doesn't know whether to
ignore her or kiss her. But Shania knows.
It's going to take a carefully crafted lesson plan
to tutor this cowboy in love.*

Read on for a sneak preview of
The Lawman's Romance Lesson,
the next great book in USA TODAY *bestselling author
Marie Ferrarella's* Forever, Texas *miniseries.*

Shania flushed as she raised her eyes toward Daniel. "I don't usually babble like this."

Daniel found the pink hue that had suddenly risen to her cheeks rather sweet. The next second, he realized that he was staring. Daniel forced himself to look away. "I hadn't noticed."

"Yes, you had," Shania contradicted. "But I think that it's very nice of you to pretend that you hadn't." When she heard Daniel laugh softly to himself, she asked him, "What's so funny?" before she could think to stop herself.

"I'm not accustomed to hearing the word *nice* used to describe me," he admitted.

Didn't the man have any close friends? Someone to bolster him up when he was down on himself? "You're kidding."

The lopsided smile answered her before he did. "Something else I'm not known for."

She pretended that he was a student and she did a quick assessment of the man before her. "You know you're being very hard on yourself."

"Not hard," he contradicted. "Just honest."

She had no intention of letting this slide. If he had been one of her students, she would have done what she could to raise his spirits—or maybe it was his self-esteem that needed help.

"Well, I think you're nice—and you do have a sense of humor."

"If you say so," Daniel replied, not about to dispute the matter. He had a feeling that arguing with Shania would be pointless. "But just so you know, I'm not about to chuck my career and become a stand-up comedian."

She grinned at his words. "See, I told you that you had a sense of humor," she declared happily.

Don't miss
The Lawman's Romance Lesson *by Marie Ferrarella,*
available April 2019 wherever
Harlequin® *Special Edition books and ebooks are sold.*

www.Harlequin.com

Get 4 FREE REWARDS!

We'll send you 2 FREE Books plus 2 FREE Mystery Gifts.

Harlequin® Special Edition books feature heroines finding the balance between their work life and personal life on the way to finding true love.

FREE
Value Over
$20

SPECIAL EXCERPT FROM

HQN™

*Read on for a sneak peek at
the first heartwarming book in Lee Tobin McClain's
Safe Haven series,* Low Country Hero!

They'd both just turned back to their work when a familiar loud, croaking sound cut the silence.

The twins shrieked and ran from where they'd been playing into the little cabin's yard and slammed into Anna, their faces frightened.

"What was that?" Anna sounded alarmed, too, kneeling to hold and comfort both girls.

"Nothing to be afraid of," Sean said, trying to hold back laughter. "It's just egrets. Type of water bird." He located the source of the sound, then went over to the trio, knelt beside them, and pointed through the trees and growth.

When the girls saw the stately white birds, they gasped.

"They're so pretty!" Anna said.

"Pretty?" Sean chuckled. "Nobody from around here would get excited about an egret, nor think it's especially pretty." But as he watched another one land beside the first, white wings spread wide as it skidded into the shallow water, he realized that there was beauty there. He just hadn't noticed it before.

That was what kids did for you: made you see the world through their fresh, innocent eyes. A fist of longing clutched inside his chest.

The twins were tugging at Anna's shirt now, trying to get her to take them over toward the birds. "You may go look as long as you can see me," she said, "but take careful steps by the water." She took the bolder twin's face in her hands. "The water's not deep, but I still don't want you to wade in. Do you understand?"

Both little girls nodded vigorously.

They ran off and she watched for a few seconds, then turned back to her work with a barely audible sigh.

"Go take a look with them," he urged her. "It's not every day kids see an egret for the first time."

"You're sure?"

"Go on." He watched her run like a kid over to her girls. And then he couldn't resist walking a few steps closer and watching them, shielded by the trees and brush.

The twins were so excited that they weren't remembering to be quiet. "It caught a *fish*!" the one was crowing, pointing at the bird, which, indeed, held a squirming fish in its mouth.

"That one's neck is like an S!" The quieter twin squatted down, rapt.

Anna eased down onto the sandy beach, obviously unworried about her or the girls getting wet or dirty, laughing and talking to them and sharing their excitement.

The sight of it gave him a melancholy twinge. His own mom had been a nature lover. She'd taken him and his brothers fishing, visited a nature reserve a few times, back in Alabama where they'd lived before coming here.

Oh, if things were different, he'd run with this, see where it led…

Don't miss
Lee Tobin McClain's Low Country Hero,
available March 2019 from HQN Books!

www.Harlequin.com

PHLTMEXP0319